Partners in the Wilderness

Travis's Choice

Ed Kienzle

JETBAK Publishing
Cheyenne, Wyoming

First printing 2002

ISBN 0-9713683-1-7 (hardcover)
      0-9713683-2-5 (paperback)

LCCN 2001133103

ATTENTION CORPORATIONS, UNIVERSITIES, COLLEGES, AND PROFESSIONAL ORGANIZATIONS: Quantity discounts are available on bulk purchases of this book for educational, gift purposes, or as premiums for increasing magazine subscriptions or renewals. Special books or book excerpts can also be created to fit specific needs. For information, please contact JETBAK Publishing, 1829 Bluegrass Circle, Cheyenne, WY 82009.

CHAPTER 1

Mrs. Goodman said, "Travis Driskoll, will you please pay attention? I will ask you again, what is an isthmus?"

Travis awoke from his daydream and said, "Oh, ah, an isthmus is a narrow strip of land where elk migrate." The rest of the class roared with laughter. They all knew what Travis had been daydreaming about, but then, so did Mrs. Goodman.

Mrs. Goodman had been growing very impatient with Travis's constant daydreaming in school. It wasn't that he was a bad student, he just had a lot on his mind these days. He thought to himself, "Yes! The year has finally come!" There would be no more hearing that he wasn't big enough or he wasn't old enough. This year, he was really going along!

Eight days ago he had reminded his father that both of his older brothers had gotten to go on the wilderness hunt when they were twelve and that, since he was now twelve, he should be allowed to go along this time. Travis had expected his father to say no. The boy couldn't even finish his dinner when his father said "Yes." He had expected to hear a "No" or a "Maybe" or "I'll think about it," but in all of his hours of preparation for this moment, he had never expected to hear a plain and simple "Yes." The boy was awestruck! It should not have been this easy. The skinny blonde-headed boy had spent weeks preparing arguments and reasons why he should be allowed to go, and he didn't even need them!

This was perhaps the happiest moment in the young boy's life. His blue eyes lit up as bright as the sun on a clear mountain morning. All he could think was, "I'm going!" He ran to the phone to call his best friend, Hal, and tell him the great news. Hal and Travis did everything together. They had been best friends for as long as either of them could remember, and had shared many great adventures together. Yes, the two boys were almost inseparable—the best kind of friends.

Hal's mom answered, and it was when she went to call him to the phone that Travis realized for the first time that he would not be sharing this adventure with his closest companion. The thought saddened Travis, but he knew that there was no sense in asking if Hal could go along. His father would never consent to taking a friend. There was no use making him mad by even asking. The subject would never be brought up. Things were going too well to do something dumb and mess them up now.

When Hal got to the phone and said "Hello" it took Travis a minute before he could speak. On the second "Hello" he blurted out, "We're going! I can't believe it, but we're going!"

Hal knew what Travis was talking about. He said, "That's great! I sure wish I was going with you." If a person could ever feel happy and sad at the same time, this was it. Both boys felt it, but they both knew that the reality was that Travis was going and Hal was not. Hal was disappointed, but he would not convey that feeling to Travis.

The boys discussed it for a few minutes and then Travis said, "We can talk about it more on the bus in the morning," and hung up the phone. Now the planning would begin.

It was about eight o'clock that evening when Travis's father came in from doing chores. He hollered for Travis and said, "We have a lot of work to do in the next eight days, and I'm gonna need a lot of help from you. I have two small jobs to finish up and I'll have to work some long hours to get them done. It will be up to you to get the tack and supplies ready to go."

All Travis could say was "Okay." He had never found it so easy to take on this much hard work. But then, he didn't regard this as work. It was much better than that! He felt as though it was an honor for him, a mere twelve-year-old, to be given so much responsibility. He also knew that his father had an ability that only fathers seem to have. He could always talk Travis into agreeing to do chores or work that he didn't really want to do. He could make the simplest things seem very important and, for a trip that would be fifteen to twenty miles into the rugged Wyoming wilderness, simple things were very important.

Of course, Travis knew the first thing to do was to make a list. He had pen and paper in hand and even had a pot of coffee ready when his dad sat down and said, "Let's get started. You will have to ride Buck, Skeeter, Annie, Dusty, and Flick every night after school. Maybe Hal can help you. The horses are in pretty good shape, but the mountains are tough on them. The better the condition the horses are in when we leave, the better they will do on the trip."

"Okay," said Travis. "That sounds easy enough. Hal and I will do it."

"You'll have to get out a pack saddle and two sets of panniers. Clean 'em up and get 'em ready to go. We'll need bridles, halters, breast collars, lead ropes, and a tie down for Skeeter." Skeeter was a good horse, but he was a bit high strung and threw his head around sometimes. The tie down would help control that. "Tomorrow on my way home from work, I'll stop at the feed store and get some oats and molasses bagged for the horses."

"I'll get the tent out," said Travis. "It will be clean and ready to go."

"Good. While you're at it, get the box of camping gear out of the shed and into the garage. We have to go through it to see if we need to replenish any of the supplies. Oh, yeah, don't forget we'll need a lot of rope, some small cotton or nylon and some half-inch manila. There's a new roll in the barn. Make sure we have a couple hundred feet. One thing's for sure, a guy never has too much rope in the wilderness."

"I'll get most of this done tomorrow after school. Hal will help me," said Travis.

"Well, if you think of anything else that we may need, just add it to your list," said Dad. "That list may get pretty long before we leave."

"I will. We won't forget anything. We'll be prepared."

"It's gettin' late and you have school tomorrow, so ya better clean up and hit the hay."

Travis said, "Okay," even though getting to bed and going to sleep were not priorities on his list of things to do. He wanted to start getting things ready for the trip right now, but this was one time he was not going to protest or disobey his father.

Travis lay in his bed unable to go to sleep. There were too many thoughts going through his mind. He was imagining everything about the trip. He tried to imagine what the great mountain man, John Colter, had felt like when he first discovered the territory they would be traveling into. Travis wished he had been living in the 1800s so that he could have traveled this country and experienced it with his idol. No school! No work! No chores! Just hunting and exploring! In his mind he could see the blue sky, the huge colorful mountainsides, and even the majestic elk.

CHAPTER 2

If there is such a thing as eternal night, Travis was sure that this night was it. He had been lying in bed for hours and had not slept for even one minute. Too many things were running through his mind. The excitement and anticipation kept his imagination going nonstop. Finally he did doze off, but even then he kept dreaming about the trip. He awakened often, tossing and turning and feeling tired, but not sleepy.

At six forty-five his mother called, "Travis, time to get up!" He heard her right away and wondered if he had been sleeping or awake when she had called. It didn't really matter, but for the first time all night he wanted to just lie in bed and relax for a while. His body said, "I'm tired," but his mind said, "Let's go!" There were things to be done and people to talk to—especially his friends. He had to tell everyone the news.

He jumped out of bed and started getting ready for school. It usually took two or three wake-up calls to get Travis out of bed in the morning, so his mom was utterly shocked when she started up the stairs for the second call and met Travis on his way down. "A little excited today, are we?" she commented as he buzzed by. "The cereal and toast are on the table."

"Okay," he said.

"Your father had to leave early for work today. He said that you should feed the horses and calves before you go to school." Travis started to pout, but his mother stopped him. "Travis, you know this is an important trip for your father, too. He's been waiting several months for you to ask permission to go. I know you two don't agree about a lot of things. He disapproves of your careless behavior and your indifferent attitude toward work. But he does love you and he wants to go on this trip, perhaps even more than you do. I really think that you should make a better effort to help out with the chores around here. Don't always be so quick to pout and make excuses about why you shouldn't have to do something. Please, just try, Dear."

Travis's mom was a short, petite, blonde-headed woman, and she was very kind. This morning the words she had with Travis were about as stern as she could be. She wasn't angry, she was just being direct. This was for Travis's own benefit and he knew it. His dad could be a very bullheaded, short-tempered person, mainly with Travis. Mom knew that if Travis didn't work hard enough to get ready to go, in one flash of anger the whole trip would be called off. She really felt that the two needed some time together to learn to like and respect each other.

Travis nodded his head in agreement. He understood, and knew what he should do. But somehow there was always that slight resistance to work—an urge to pout and procrastinate rather than to just do something and get it done. His dad always told him that if he would put half as much time and effort into doing his chores as he did trying to get out of them, he would have much more time to play and goof around.

Travis gulped down a bowl of cereal and headed for the barn to feed the calves and horses. On his way out, Mom called after him, "Hurry, so you won't be late for school."

On his way to the barn, Travis imagined how grand it would be to come home from the trip with the largest bull elk anybody in this county had ever seen. He knew that they would do it. Even though his dad had not shot anything on any of his hunting trips since his brothers had left home, Travis was convinced that this one would be a success. How could it fail? Dad would have the great hunter, Travis Driskoll, with him this time. If Dad couldn't get it done, Travis was positive that he, himself, could. Even though he was not yet old enough to shoot game, he could show his dad a thing or two! He had studied every magazine printed on how to hunt elk successfully in the Rocky Mountains. He had read all of the books in the school library about elk and their habitat. He was sure that he was the most knowledgeable person on earth about elk.

He had thought of nothing else for weeks. It was as though the thoughts possessed him. He came out of his daydream as he reached the barn door. For a moment, he had to struggle to remember what he was supposed to do. "Oh, yes," he thought to himself, "feed the horses and calves." He crawled up into the hayloft and opened the door above the corral. Flick and Skeeter came running. They knew what was going on and were usually the first ones to the hay.

Travis struggled with the heavy alfalfa bales. They weighed practically as much as he did. When he finally got one up to the door, he cut the twines and started to kick the hay out for the horses. Alfalfa leaves scattered everywhere. Skeeter's back was covered with the tiny green specks. After he had dragged one more bale and tossed it down for the horses, Travis fed the calves. Without wasting any time, he headed back toward the house as fast as he could run. There was no way he was going to be late for the bus today!

Travis quickly washed and changed his shoes. He hollered goodbye to his mom as he ran to the end of the driveway. Hal was already on the bus when Travis got on. Travis rushed to the back seat where they always met.

"So, when ya leavin'?" Hal asked.

"The first of October," Travis replied.

"Not too far off, is it?"

"No!"

"Hope you have a great trip."

"I will. I only wish you could come along."

"I know, but my parents wouldn't let me go anyhow. Enough of this," said Hal. "Let's not talk about me not going. Let's talk about getting you ready to go."

"Okay," said Travis, "but it won't be easy. Dad's got a ton of work to finish up. He was wondering if you could help me some with the horses and the tack."

"Sure could! I'll call home to see if I can get off the bus at your house tonight. We'll start right away."

Neither of the boys had said a word to another soul on the bus, but within ten minutes everybody knew. The word had spread quickly from one seat to the next. Most of the kids didn't care much about the fact that Travis was going hunting, but they were envious that he would get to miss six days of school right before fall break.

Travis had told Hal about all of the chores his father had given him to do, and they were trying to decide what they should do first when the bus arrived at school. The two boys were the last to get off, and by this time it appeared that the entire school knew about the trip. Travis was the center of attention everywhere he went. All he talked about was camping, horses, and elk. It was endless, but Travis didn't get tired of it at all. He was enjoying the attention so much that it led him to do a bit of bragging. "We are going to bring home the hugest bull elk you have ever seen!" he proclaimed on the playground that first morning.

When the bell rang, Travis headed for his classroom and, for the first time, he felt some anxiety about the trip. He had totally forgotten about Mrs. Goodman. Surely she knew about the trip by now, and Travis wondered what kind of trouble she was going to cause. What would she say? Would she chew him out and tell him that this sort of thing was not necessary for the education of a young boy? Worse yet, would she call up his dad and make him change his mind about taking Travis?

Class started and went on through the day, just like any other day. Mrs. Goodman never said a word, other than to ask Travis to stop talking and pay attention several times. She never once mentioned the trip, and he was certainly not going to bring up the subject. After all, she might be waiting for him to do just that. No, sir! He wasn't born yesterday. He would not fall into one of the teacher's sinister plots.

When the final bell rang, Travis and Hal ran for the bus as though that would get them home faster. It seemed like eternity before the bus was loaded and left the school. The pair had never waited so long for anything and, when the bus door opened at the end of the quarter-mile long driveway, the two boys sprinted for the house.

Travis's mom met them in the kitchen with sandwiches and juice. She said, "I talked to your mother, Hal. You can spend the night here."

"Great!" roared Hal.

"Do either of you have homework?"

"No," they said in unison, and they grabbed sandwiches and headed out the door. They decided to ride and exercise the horses first, since they had determined that to be the most important task they had been given.

They saddled Skeeter and Annie, which was a job in itself for two twelve-year-old boys. Skeeter was a tall, high-strung sorrel, and he didn't like standing still to be saddled and bridled. He was part thoroughbred and part quarter horse. Dad always said, "The thoroughbred blood makes him dancy, and the quarter horse blood makes him tough." He wasn't mean. He just couldn't stand still.

Annie was quite different. She was short for a quarter horse, stocky, black, and gentle as a six-week-old puppy. All of this made her a lot easier than Skeeter to saddle. The boys put lead ropes on Buck, Flicka, and Dusty. They were going to be pack horses for this trip, and they needed exercise, too.

Travis said, "I'll lead Buck and Flick. You take Dusty."

"Sounds good," said Hal.

"Let's head out to the west pasture and ride the hills."

"Okay. But not too fast to start with."

The boys walked the horses for about the first half mile, and then they trotted, and finally galloped them for about twenty minutes. The horses were starting to sweat up pretty good when the boys decided to head home. By the time they got back to the barn, it was nearly dark.

Travis asked Hal to unsaddle, brush down, and water the horses while he kicked a couple of bales down out of the hayloft for them. Then he started to gather some of the equipment for the trip.

"If I don't get some of these things in the garage before Dad gets home, he'll be mad, and I'm not going to let that happen! I promised Mom I wouldn't. We shouldn't have ridden so long. Tomorrow the ride will be shorter. Let's hurry!"

"Okay."

"I'll meet you in the garage," and Travis disappeared into the shed, which also served as an excess tack room. All of the camping and hunting supplies were kept there. The old shed didn't have lights, so Travis had to feel around for the box. Finally he located it and started pulling on it. It was heavier than he had anticipated. He had looked through it many times, but he had never tried to move it before. It was a race against time. He had said that he would have it in the garage, and here it was dark and he could barely move the box alone. If he didn't get it to the garage, he would be a failure in the eyes of his father one more time.

Just as he got it yanked out of the shed and realized it was so heavy he wouldn't be able to get it to the garage in an hour, much less in a few minutes, the lights in the barn went off.

Travis hollered, "Hal, over here!" Hal came running. "Quick! Grab ahold and help me."

The two pulled the box with relative ease and, within a few minutes, were in the garage with it. "Quick, get a flashlight from Mom," said Travis.

Hal was back in an instant.

"Let's go get the rest of the tack out of the shed."

The boys ran now and, within minutes, had a pack saddle and panniers in the garage. They were exhausted when Mom stuck her head out the door and called, "Suppertime!"

● CHAPTER 3 ●

The next six days were busy. The two boys worked each night to get things ready for the trip. Travis could hardly believe it. He was going to miss a whole week of school! He had never been allowed to do such a thing before in his whole life. But, as his father said, the trip would be educational. He would be learning a lot about animals and nature.

The final days at school had been long. Minutes seemed like hours and hours like days, but finally Travis was down to his last afternoon. Mrs. Goodman still had not said a word about the trip, not even when Travis had brought a note from home explaining why he would be missing school. It just wasn't like her. She hadn't given him any extra homework or lectured him about absences or anything. Deep down inside, he was a bit worried that she might still do something to stop his trip. He had made it to last recess and the students were all getting ready to go out and play when she called his name. "Travis! Could I speak to you for a moment?"

Travis thought, "Oh, no! Has she called home and stopped the trip? How could she do such a thing? It's just not fair. It's all over. This is cruel." As he walked toward her desk, he thought Mrs. Goodman seemed to be taking a bit too much pleasure in the demise of his trip. How could she do this to him?

Then she spoke. "I hope you have a very good time on your trip. I generally do not approve of a student missing a whole week of school like this but, after talking to your parents, I think it will be okay."

Travis sighed with relief and even smiled faintly as he said, "Thanks!"

Mrs. Goodman continued, "Your assignment will be to keep a daily journal of your trip. It will be for a grade, and I want it to be as good as

I know you are capable of doing. Be thorough and be descriptive. Write about what happens each day, and describe what you see. All you will need is a notebook and a pencil."

The directions seemed to go on forever and ever. Travis only heard about half of them as he was thinking all along, "I get to go! Yes! Yes! Yes! I get to go!"

He had heard enough, though, that he thought he knew what to do, and when she asked, "Do you understand your assignment?" he nodded.

"Okay, you may go out for recess now."

Recess and the rest of the afternoon went by very quickly. Travis wondered if Mrs. Goodman had been putting off talking to him about the trip on purpose to make him squirm and suffer, or if she had some other motive. One thing was for sure, though. He was not going to ask her until after the trip.

When the final bell rang, Mrs. Goodman walked up to him and gave him a big hug. She told him to take care of himself, and to be very careful. She had never hugged him before, and it was almost embarrassing to him but he said, "Okay." Then he ran for the bus.

Hal jabbed him on the arm and said, "Nice hug, Dude." He chuckled. "A real live grizzly bear hug!"

Once again all thoughts were on the trip and elk hunting. Travis told Hal he would be the first one to be called when he and his dad got home with the mighty bull elk. Travis proclaimed to everybody on the bus that he would bring home the big bull, not some young raghorn with small antlers that would run and hide from a large trophy bull. "They're not big enough, smart enough, or experienced enough to even be a challenge. Anyone can get a raghorn, the smallest of bulls. My bull will be at least a six point, probably even a seven point world record!" It was his last chance to brag before he got home, because he knew that his father would never stand for such talk. He would surely not brag around him!

Travis was the center of attention during the ride home. He bragged and boasted practically all the way. But there was a moment of silence when he once again realized Hal was not going with them. Travis said with despair in his voice, "I sure wish you were going along, Hal."

Hal said, "I know that, but let's not talk about it. We have too much to do tonight to get you ready to go in the morning. Talking about it is senseless anyhow." Travis could feel the disappointment in Hal's voice and changed the subject.

When the bus stopped at the Driskoll's driveway, the boys bailed out and raced to the house. Hal won. But, of course, he always won. He was a much faster runner than Travis.

When they got to the house, Travis's mom said, "Your dad will probably be late. He said that you would know what to do to get ready." Travis knew there was a lot of work to do and, as quickly as the two had entered the house, they left it.

The boys packed all of the camping gear, tack, and food. Then they fed the horses. They had just gassed up the pickup when Mr. Driskoll came driving in from work. As he got out of his truck he spotted the boys by the barn and shouted, "Is everything ready to go?"

In unison, they shouted back, "Yeah!" Matt Driskoll smiled and walked into the house.

After dinner, they discussed what still needed to be done and determined that everything that was left could be finished up in the morning. Finally, Travis's dad announced, "It's about time for you guys to hit the sack. We need to get an early start in the morning."

The two boys lay awake for half of the night talking about elk and trying to prove to each other who was the better outdoorsman and elk expert. They talked and laughed for hours. Then suddenly Hal said in a concerned voice, "You know, old man Wick got attacked by a bear last year . . ."

Travis had forgotten about the bear until now. He responded, "Yeah. Heard he had 360 stitches from that. I'm not worried about that, though. My dad's been an outfitter. He's had some encounters with bears and he knows what to do."

Both boys remained quiet for a few minutes. Then they began to talk about elk again. By the time they finally fell asleep, each boy was convinced that he was the foremost expert, and that he had proven it with his own expertise and superior knowledge.

CHAPTER 4

Morning came too soon, but on first call the boys were out of bed and ready to go. They gulped down breakfast before daylight and ran out the door to help finish loading, only to find that it was all done. Travis thought, "Dad must be as excited to go as I am."

Matt stepped out from the opposite side of the horse trailer and roared, "Are you ready to go? I am."

Then Travis knew. "Yeah, he's as excited as I am."

"Go tell your mom we're leaving."

Travis ran to the house and hollered, "We're leaving, Mom!"

She replied, "Not before I get hugs and kisses."

They stood out by the pickup and said their goodbyes. Mom almost cried as she hugged Travis and told him goodbye. She said, "You behave, be careful, and listen to your father. No matter what you think, he is the expert. He's been there before and it's dangerous country and, if I don't stop now, I may not let you go. I love you very much. You be careful. I'll see you in two weeks." She gave Travis another big hug and opened the pickup door for him.

She then walked around the front of the pickup and gave Dad a long kiss and said, "Take good care of my baby, and you be careful as well. Have fun. I love you." With that final "I love you," Matt was in the driver's seat and they were ready to go.

Hal hollered, "Have fun, and get a big one!" Both boys were feeling disappointment that Hal was not coming along, but they tried not to show it. It was silent as they started to drive off. Then Travis stuck his head out of the window and hollered, "I'll call you as soon as I get back!"

Travis's disappointment didn't last too long as he started thinking about the glorious days ahead. He had studied all of the maps and, as near as he could tell, the trailhead was about 205 miles from his house. He was imagining heading up the trail when his father said, "You know, I'm really proud of you. For a long time I've thought that you wouldn't want to go on this trip because it would be too much work. But you proved me wrong, and I'm so proud of you. It's amazing! I thought you'd probably want to go at first, but once the work started, you'd change your mind. I guess you're growin' up, ha, Son."

Travis smiled and said, "Yeah."

"I do have to say, though, the work has just begun and, like your mom said, it's big country that we're goin' to. It's beautiful, but it's equally dangerous. We'll have to be able to depend on each other. When I ask you or tell you to do something, I expect you to do it. I'm not mad or anything. It's just important that you understand and listen. It could mean the difference between life and death."

Travis listened carefully as his father was talking, partly because of the serious tone of his voice, and partly because he understood how important this lecture was. It had to be important for his father to spend so much time telling him how to behave. All of this talk was coming from a quiet man who often didn't say fifty words in an entire day. The seriousness made Travis very attentive. He wondered if his brothers had gotten this same lecture once they were on the road, or if this were a special one prepared just for him. He decided it didn't really matter. He had better just listen.

Finally his father was finished and there was silence in the truck. Neither of them had spoken a word for about ten minutes when Dad asked, with a grin, "Just how big is this monster bull that we're going to get? I hear around town that it's going to be the biggest one ever killed in the whole county."

Travis winced. He knew that there was a bragging lecture coming on. Instead, all his dad said was, "I was just kind of wanting to know so's I wouldn't shoot one that was too small." Matt smiled and knew that his point was made.

The lack of sleep was catching up to Travis and he dozed off in the truck. His dreams were about elk and being aboard the horses in the mountains. They were grand dreams, the kind where everything is perfect. The dreams lived up to Travis's highest expectations for the trip.

In his sleep, Travis's head had slid over against the window and it began to bounce against the glass whenever the pickup tires hit rough spots on the road. It was the annoyance of his head hitting the window that finally woke him up. He was surprised to see a winding uphill road with trees on either side. He thought to himself, "Must have been asleep for hours." He looked over at his dad and smiled. The tension was building. If they were in the mountains, then they must be getting very close. "Where are we?" he asked.

His father replied, "We're in the mountains, Sonny!" in a teasing manner.

"I know we're in the mountains. But where in the mountains are we?"

"Well, we're just about to the top. We'll reach the divide here in a few minutes."

Now Travis knew where they were. The mention of the Continental Divide always sparked curiosity in his mind. He knew that the divide was the spot where water on one side went to the Pacific Ocean and water on the other side went to the Atlantic. He had always wondered, if he took a jug of water and walked to the top, whether he could find the exact spot where the water would flow both directions. He had been up this highway many times going to Jackson or Yellowstone Park, and each time he had this same curious thought. His father had told him about a creek in the wilderness called Two Ocean Creek. He had said that the creek came down a mountain and split at a place called The Parting of the Waters to form two creeks, Atlantic and Pacific Creeks. Each, of course, flowed toward its respective ocean.

He sat imagining what the Parting of the Waters would look like. He was thinking about asking if they could go see it when he noticed the green highway sign. It said *Continental Divide*. Travis turned and spoke. "Suppose we could haul some water up there and find the exact spot where the water runs both ways?"

His dad laughed and replied, "I don't know. We might have to try it someday though. It's funny you'd mention that, Son. I've thought that very same thought every time I've ever come over this mountain. I guess some day we'll have to drag some water up that hill and see if we can. Long ways up, though. I guess you'll carry the water, huh?"

Travis laughed and said, "Maybe."

By this time they had gone over Togwottee Mountain Pass and were headed downhill. The road was steep and full of curves. It seemed to be as much a chore now to keep the pickup slowed down as it had been to keep the speed up coming up the other side. The sun was high in the perfectly clear blue sky, and only in the tallest wooded areas was there any shade on the road. The weather was just right for starting a pack trip.

The pickup finally came to the bottom of the mountain and, once again, the motor had to work to pull the load. They were approaching a KOA when Matt said, "This is your last chance. Can you think of anything we need?"

Travis said, "No," but they slowed down and pulled into the small campground convenience store anyway.

"I think we need something," Dad said.

"What?" asked Travis.

"Well, this is the last modern conveniences we're gonna see for two weeks. I think I could go for some fries, a burger, and a huge milkshake. How about you?"

Travis didn't hesitate. He just said, "Yeah," with a big grin on his face. He was in a hurry to get to the trailhead, but the food sounded pretty good to him.

The two gobbled down their food and, in no time, were back on the road. Anticipation and excitement were growing. Travis felt butterflies in his stomach, knowing that there were only a few miles to go. He couldn't wait to get started up the trail. Yet, for the first time, he was experiencing some hesitation, maybe even some fear. He was wondering what would happen if he got hurt or sick. He remembered what Hal had said about the bear attacking old man Wick. He rationalized to himself that his father would take care of him. Dad would take care of him, no matter what. Matt Driskoll was an expert outdoorsman. He had run into many situations with other hunters getting sick or injured when he had been an outfitter years ago. Still, there was some uncertainty that Travis couldn't seem to shake off.

As he was mulling this over in his mind, his father asked, "What's wrong? You're so deep in thought."

Travis shrugged it off. He didn't really want to tell his father what the problem was. He finally replied, "Just thinkin' about the elk."

"Yeah, we'll see elk, Son. Now there are some things I need to remind you about. I know I've said it before, but you absolutely have to listen to me. If I say something, you pay attention. If I tell you to do something, you do it. You stay with me at all times and never wander off. You could get lost or slip and fall. Lots of things could happen. There are grizzly out here, and it's just a huge country. We're going to be a lot of miles from nowhere, and we're a team. We depend on each other. I'm not trying to scare you or anything. I just want us both to be safe and have a fun time. You understand me?"

"Yeah," Travis replied. "I'll do my best, Dad. I won't mess up!"

Dad's speech had not eased Travis's feeling of apprehension. It had only made it worse. But he was smart enough to know that that was half of his father's intention. He was sure that he would receive at least a few more of these lectures in the days to come.

They were finally crossing Pacific Creek. It was only a few more miles to the trailhead!

CHAPTER 5

The trailhead was not what Travis had expected. He didn't really know what it would look like, but he thought it would be isolated and very grand, something like in a movie. But it was just a cow trail going out the end of a meadow with a few small willows and aspens scattered through it. There were some small outbuildings or outhouses. It reminded him of a vacant campground.

As the pickup came to a stop, Travis opened his door to hear the sound of running water. The creek was down below them somewhere and, even though he couldn't see it, Travis could tell by the sound of flowing water that it was not far away. The air was brisk and fresh, and there was a slight breeze, just enough to cause a few of the golden aspen leaves to start floating toward the ground. It was autumn in the mountains.

Matt came around the trailer and said, "I'm gonna back the horses out now. You take them down to the creek one at a time for water. Give them a good drink, but not too much. We'll be crossing creeks along the trail and they can drink more then. As you bring them back, I'll start packing them."

Travis said, "Okay," and took Dusty's lead rope as he came out of the trailer. He didn't ask about how to get to the creek. He just started leading the horse toward the sound of the running water. Heading straight for the creek turned out to be probably not the best choice. The boy and horse went down a small draw and disappeared into some willows. When they cleared the willows, Travis could see the creek, but they would have to go through about twenty feet of bog to get there. The ground was soft, but Travis led Dusty out into it anyway. About halfway through the mud, the horse sank in to his knees. He immediately snorted, jumped, and continued crow-hopping until he was on the rocky creek bank. Travis had let go of the lead rope, and now he scrambled to catch up to the horse. Luckily for him, Dusty was thirsty and Travis caught him right at the river bank with his nose in the icy cold mountain water.

Although he didn't realize it at the time, Travis had learned a very valuable lesson about things that can happen if you get reckless or careless in the mountains. When Dusty was finished drinking, the pair walked down the creek bank until they came to a trail that led up to the road. This route was much easier, and safer, too!

When the boy and horse got back to the pickup, Dad had all of the tack and supplies unloaded and sorted out beside the different pack saddles on the ground. He said, "Tie him up here and I'll saddle and pack him. You can water Buck and Flick next. Yup, pack horses first. If we hurry, we can make six or seven miles before dark."

"I'll hurry," said Travis as he headed for the creek again.

The rest of the watering went without incident, except for Skeeter. When Travis led him down to the water, he cocked his ears back and jerked and pulled away from the running water. He was scared of it and apparently not too thirsty, either. Travis tried to lead him up to the water a half-dozen times, but each time Skeeter snorted and jerked back away from the creek. Finally Travis gave up and led the horse back to the trail.

"Skeeter's scared of the creek. He wouldn't drink," Travis reported to his father.

"That's okay. We have to cross Whetstone Creek about two or three miles up the trail. We can get him a drink there. He'll be thirsty by then."

By this time, Dad had pack saddles on Dusty and Flick, and even had them loaded. They were both tall, strong, heavy-boned horses, ideal for packing in the mountains. Travis inspected the loads as his father worked at packing Buck. Dusty was a bay color. He would pack in the feed, the tent, and a few of the camping supplies. Flick was a huge palomino colored horse. He would carry the groceries, camping gear, and bed rolls.

Travis was staring up the mountainside across the creek, dreaming about elk again when he heard his father say, "We could probably get up the trail a ways today if a guy could get a little help around here!"

Travis responded and went to help saddle Skeeter and Annie. He hoped his father was joking, but he wasn't sure about it. He wasn't smiling, but that was Dad's way. He often pretended to be coarse or growly when, deep down inside, he had to fight to keep from cracking a smile. All the same, he wasn't smiling now. Travis wasn't sure, and that's the way Dad liked it!

Matt threw a saddle up on Annie and said, "Cinch it down tight, Bud, and I'll get Skeeter." Bud was a nickname for Travis that was used only by his dad. "Get the cinch as tight as you can, and remember to check it once in a while. We don't want you turning upside down going up the trail. The scenery isn't very good from down there, and the elk are surely harder than heck to see with your nose stuck in the dirt!" He chuckled and walked off.

Finally all of the horses were saddled and packed, and there was only one thing left to do. That was to get the rifles out and put them in the scabbards. Travis knew that his dad would be carrying a 300 magnum in his scabbard, and Travis would carry a 25-06 in his. Dad had told him that he was not to touch the gun. It was only intended to be used as a backup rifle in case something happened to the 300 mag. He had told Travis about a time when he was younger and had his rifle in a scabbard on a horse. He and some friends were packing up a steep hill when the horse he was riding lost its footing. The horse reared and tipped over backward, breaking the stock on the hunting rifle as he fell. After that, he always carried a backup.

Travis wasn't sure, but he wondered why his father had chosen the 25-06 as a backup. It was a smaller caliber than several of the rifles he had left at home. Travis thought maybe he had brought it just in case Travis needed a rifle. It didn't matter right now, though, and he was not going to ask. At least, not yet.

With the rifles in the scabbards, Dad had only to strap the 44 magnum pistol to his hip and they would be ready to go. He called the 44 mag his "bear protection." The pistol was not as powerful as the rifles but, if a hunter's horse was scared by a bear, especially a grizzly, and threw the rider to the ground, he would at least have some short range protection.

This was no laughing matter to Matt Driskoll. He had been charged by a grizzly before. Travis had heard stories about the attack, and he figured he would hear more of them at some point on this trip.

With everything loaded, the two now only had to climb up on their horses and they were off!

CHAPTER 6

As soon as they left the meadow and entered the tall pine forest, the trail became everything Travis had imagined it would be. Only now it was real! He could feel it as well as see it. His anxiety was forgotten, and he only wanted to ride on and see more.

The trail ran parallel to Pacific Creek through heavy timber on a bench about 50 yards above the creek. Travis was paying very close attention to the trail as it ran only a few feet away from the drop-off going down to the creek. Annie was a calm mannered, surefooted horse, but Travis knew that not even an elk would attempt walking down to the creek in this area. He was sure he didn't want to ride down there either! There was a huge mountain towering over them on the other side of the creek. Travis had to lay his head back and bend backward to see the top of the mountain above the creek. It was only about one o'clock in the afternoon, yet the heavy timber was dark like dusk on a rainy day.

The group pressed on up the trail almost always climbing, but not a steep climb. Matt led all three of the pack horses behind him while Travis and Annie brought up the rear. They rode in and out of the timber alongside the creek for several miles. Each time they passed through one of the sunny meadows, Travis would watch closely for elk or signs of any type of wildlife which might have been bedded down or feeding there the previous night.

The lack of sign in the meadows was a bit discouraging, but still Travis dreamt on. Elk were on his mind. He envisioned huge bulls with their harems, fighting off intruding bulls wishing to steal their cows. It was an excellent daydream, with bulls whistling, bugling, and grunting to show their dominance over the herd.

It was then that Travis realized that he had never actually heard a live bull elk bugle. He had heard them on television and in videos, but never in the wild. He wondered if he would even recognize the sound of a live bull bugling. He sure hoped he would!

Suddenly, a foul, musty odor grabbed his attention and, as he looked ahead, he noticed that it had caught his father's attention, also. Travis had never smelled this odor before and he wondered if it might be a bear. He had been told that bears had a terrible smell, and this was certainly a bad odor. Instinctively, he held back his urge to holler. He just watched for a moment as his father tied Skeeter and the pack train off to a tree. This dismissed the idea of a bear. "If it had been a bear," he thought, "Dad would have been reaching to pull the rifle out of his scabbard rather than quietly tying the horses off."

Matt motioned to Travis and pointed into the trees toward the creek. Travis slowly slid down off Annie, letting the reins drop to the ground. His eyes were focused on the spot where his dad had been pointing. He couldn't see anything, but the musty pungent odor was reeking in the air. His eyes searched from tree to tree, but still he could see nothing. Slowly he moved up toward his father, crouching as he went. When he got up beside him, Dad whispered, "There's a bull elk down in the trees."

"Where?"

"I saw a patch of hide, but now I can't see him."

"Let's go down there."

"Slowly and quietly," Dad cautioned.

The two moved down through the trees, stalking as quietly as possible. Travis stepped around a tree and put his foot down dead center on a fallen twig. It popped, and the forest came to life. Patches of elk hide were flashing through the trees all over in front of them. It sounded like a herd of cattle breaking limbs and crashing timber. The elk were sure a lot noisier than Travis had expected, and quick, too!

"How many were there, Dad? Ten? Fifteen?"

"No. Maybe three. Probably small bulls. Raghorns."

"The bull I saw was pretty big . . ." and then Travis stopped. He had caught himself exaggerating, exaggerating to the point of lying. He hadn't even seen a horn. His dad gave him that look, like he wanted to say, "Don't lie to me," but he didn't say anything. The disgusted look said it all.

Travis changed the subject quickly. "What was that smell?"

"It was the elk, especially the bulls. They smell the worst this time of year, right at the end of the rut."

The two had not carried a rifle down the hill because the hunting season was not open yet. This was only Saturday, and the season didn't open until Monday. As they walked, Dad said, "You walk like an ox. Try to walk quietly. Pick your feet up."

"I was."

"No, you weren't. You were walking like an ox, dragging your feet. You have to be quiet when you're walking and hunting."

Travis didn't argue anymore. The lecture wasn't painful, and he had learned the smell of an elk. He would not forget that smell, either!

As they topped the hill, Dad said, "Pretty exciting, huh?"

"Yup."

"Just pick up your feet next time."

Travis thought, "Just let it go!" but he didn't say it.

After the cinches were tightened down and checked, they headed on up the trail. Skeeter was thirsty when they came to the next creek. He was still hesitant, but he finally did drink.

By now it was getting to be mid afternoon, and Dad thought that they would ride for about one more hour and then camp for the night. They hit some flat aspen country and Travis dug the compass out of his shirt pocket. They were heading northeast. Dad had told him to always know which direction you were going. It could end up helping you find your way back.

At about four o'clock they came to a spot where a small spring ran out of the end of a meadow. They decided this would be a good spot to spend the night. There was a good valley to glass with the spotting scope before dark and tall grass for the horses to chew on all night long.

After unloading and picketing the horses, Travis began to set up a pup tent while Matt dug a fire pit and gathered some firewood for the evening. When the work was done, they sat on the ground and relaxed for a few minutes soaking up the sun's final rays of the day.

"How are you likin' it so far, Trav?"

"It's okay," Travis replied, but then he rethought his answer and said, "It's great! It's awesome! I can't wait until Monday!"

"Yeah, Monday will be good. We'll get after 'em!" referring to the elk. "Let's set up a scope and snoop around a bit."

"Okay."

Travis ran to one of the pack saddles and grabbed a tripod and the spotting scope. They set it up and began to scan the valley below them. Dad was looking through the scope for a long time, moving it around and adjusting it. Finally he said, "There you go."

Travis looked in the scope.

"Do you see 'em?"

"Yeah," Travis replied. Three deer were moving out into a meadow to feed. It looked like a doe and two fawns. Suddenly there were five and then seven, all does and fawns. But the eighth one was a buck, and a pretty nice one as far as he could tell from three quarters of a mile away. Travis looked through the scope nonstop for about half an hour and would have continued to look, but his father jabbed him on the arm and said, "Come on. We've got one more thing to do before dark."

Travis looked up and went to follow his dad.

"Grab some rope. We gotta put the food and the horses' feed up in a tree, or we might lose it to bears."

Travis didn't say anything. He just grabbed the rope and most of the food. He dragged it over by a tall, knotty ponderosa pine that had a huge dead limb sticking out on one side. They threw ropes over the limb and hoisted the food and feed sack up high.

By now the sun had set behind their camp and, if it were not for their small campfire, there would be no light. A cloud cover had drifted in, and the blackness of the night was darker than any night Travis had ever seen. The coyotes began to howl. Dad noticed Travis grinning across the fire from him.

"What is it?"

"I was just thinkin' that they're not howling at the moon!" They both got a chuckle out of that.

After eating a little jerky, some licorice, and dried fruit, they crawled into the tent and went to bed.

CHAPTER 7

Travis slept like a rock that night. The combination of fresh mountain air, excitement about going hunting, and lack of sleep had exhausted him.

He awoke very early to the annoying sound of his father's snoring. It was pitch black outside yet, so Travis just lay in his sleeping bag wide awake and wondering what the day would bring. The snoring persisted and, even though it was annoying, Travis decided to let his dad sleep. He had remembered Mom saying that Dad only snored when he was very tired. Besides, Travis had no idea what time it was. He had not worn his watch, but right now he wished that he had. He couldn't tell if it was one o'clock in the morning or if it was closer to six o'clock. There was no way for him to know. He might think about waking Dad if he knew it was almost six. Instead, he just lay there wide awake twitching his toes, fiddling his fingers, and imagining the hunt.

Several times he heard a shrill noise outside, but he couldn't tell what it was over the loud snoring. The noise was not far away, and he figured it was a coyote that had moved closer to camp than the ones they had heard before they went to bed. The howl seemed to be getting closer and louder.

Suddenly Travis realized what the sound was! He jumped out of his sleeping bag, startling his father. He felt around for the zipper at the tent's entrance. It was still pitch black out, and it seemed to Travis as though he would never get it open. Finally he found it and yanked up on the plastic handle. As he began to bail out of the tent, his father called, "Slow down! You think you're gonna see that elk? It's pitch black out there.

Yes! What Travis had thought might be a coyote was actually a bull elk bugling, and he was really close by now! His father was right, though. He could not see a thing.

Travis sat and listened. Dad was in the tent laughing at him. Travis could hear him moving around inside. When he stuck his head out of the tent, he said, "Hand me that lantern." Travis did, and in a moment there was light.

"Pretty awesome, huh?" his dad said as he started to build a fire.

"Yeah! Must be a big one, huh, Dad?"

"You've been watching too many videos!" Dad said jokingly. "It's probably just a raghorn. One thing you'll learn out here is that you can't tell how big a bull is by its bugle. Maybe once in a while, but not always."

Travis listened. The bull bugled again. Travis thought it was the sweetest sound he had ever heard.

His father continued, "I was out one morning a long time ago when I heard the loudest, deepest bugle and grunt I had ever heard. I knew I was on a big one. Well, to make a long story short, when he stepped into sight, he was just a three by four raghorn."

Travis couldn't believe that the bull he was hearing was a raghorn, but the bugle was moving farther away now and he would probably never see the bull anyway.

It was beginning to get light now, and Dad was cooking up some breakfast. Travis was engrossed in listening for the bull. But it was gone now and there was no more bugling.

"Hey, Bud! If you're gonna ride with me today, you might want to put some pants on. Of course, you can ride in your long johns if you want to."

Travis jumped up and said, "I'll get dressed and then . . ."

But his dad cut him off. "It's gonna be pretty warm today. Maybe you want to get rid of the long johns and just wear unders!"

Travis scowled. As he crawled into the tent he thought to himself, "When did Dad become such a wise guy?"

By the time the two got everything loaded and ate breakfast, the sun was coming over the tops of the trees. It wasn't cold this morning.

There wasn't even any frost. Dad commented, "It's actually pretty warm for this time of year."

As they headed up the trail again, Travis watched for the bull that had been bugling earlier. He wanted to spot it in the worst way, more to prove his dad wrong about the size of the antlers than anything. But his earlier premonition had been correct. He would never see that bull.

CHAPTER 8

The eight miles to the camp went by quickly. The ride on this day was less eventful. The only wildlife they saw were a cow and calf moose, and a coyote. Oh, there were squirrels, chipmunks, ravens and other birds, but Travis really didn't count them. He was more interested in animals that could be hunted.

Travis had been so busy daydreaming and looking around at the countryside that he didn't even notice they had left the main trail.

They had come to Fox Park, a long, narrow meadow. Matt wanted to camp on the west end where they could catch some morning sun. He had told Travis that the time of day right around dawn was the coldest, and a man should make his camp to take advantage of the warmth the morning sun would offer. The sun would come up in the southeast. Therefore, they would camp at the northwest end of the park.

It hadn't seemed like a long ride at all to Travis, but when he crawled off Annie for the final time that day, he felt stiff and sore. The insides of his legs were especially sore from rubbing against the saddle, he guessed. It was afternoon now, and there was a lot of work to be done before dark.

The two began unloading and unpacking the horses right away. They had hardly spoken since daylight, and Travis thought his dad was behaving more like the person he knew. Today he was, once again, a man of few words. He didn't even have to tell Travis to lead the horses to water. Travis just did it.

There was a small spring bubbling out of the ground about fifty yards from camp toward the middle of the meadow. Travis decided that this would be a good spot to water the horses.

As he led Buck to water, he thought about how small the horse looked now compared to Dusty and Flick. On the trip up here, he had looked larger, but Travis realized that it was the load he carried that made him look bigger. Travis had known ever since he could remember that Buck was a short horse. Yes, it was the load. Buck had carried a huge pack which looked like it probably weighed a thousand pounds, but the pack consisted of all the clothes, sleeping bags, and light bulky things and it probably actually weighed less than two hundred pounds.

Buck, like Matt, had made this trip many times. He was an old horse and, at one time before the trip started, they had considered leaving him at home. Dad thought the trip would be hard on him. But in the end they decided to bring him anyhow. Dad had said, "Old Buck may not be much of a mount, but he's the best pack horse I've ever seen."

Travis had never packed meat before, but he had heard some good stories about how horses would go crazy when they got near a dead animal and the smell of blood. Many hunters had been hurt by horses who went ballistic when an attempt was made to load meat on them. Not Buck, though! Travis remembered a story about a time when his mom had shot a calf elk for meat and old Buck had stood with the lead rope on the ground and eaten while they put the whole quartered elk on him. The only time he moved was when he had to reach for more grass.

Travis's older brother, Jess, was along that time, and when they left the kill site Jess was leading old Buck. Jess slipped and fell down. Buck stumbled too, and stepped on Jess's ankle. It wasn't Buck's fault. It was just one of those things that happens. Dad had had to carry Jess out on his back while Buck followed behind with the elk. They came to a spot on the trail where some other hunters had left a spike. Most horses would have snorted or shied and cautiously passed the elk, but not Buck. He stopped right by it and started grazing. He was going to wait for someone to load that elk also! Dad had always said, "One elk's not enough for Buck." Travis remembered this story well. He had probably heard it a hundred times.

Buck wasn't much of a mount only because he stumbled a lot with a rider on him. No one seemed to know if it was because of poor eyesight, or if he was lazy and dragged his feet. Maybe it was because he was always looking for something to eat. It didn't really matter, though, because they had brought him along to pack meat, and he was the best at that.

Now the horses were watered and picketed, and the reminiscing was over. "Travis, you need to give each of the horses some oats," Matt said as he worked on setting up the canvas wall tent. Travis gave each horse a generous portion of the feed and headed over to help his dad set up the tent.

The tent was about ten feet wide by fifteen feet long. It had three-foot side walls and was made of white canvas. This would be their home for the rest of the hunt. It was much roomier than the pup tent, and warmer too. It had a wood stove for heating and cooking. The pair worked hard at putting the aluminum frame for the tent together. Travis was sorting and organizing the parts, and Dad was piecing them together.

"Go get the hatchet, Bud."

Travis didn't answer. He just ran to get it. One thing Travis knew was that when he was helping his dad and he needed a tool, he wanted it now, and quickly! The faster he got it, the happier his dad would be. He found it in the pile of gear and ran it back inside the tent.

"Here," Travis said.

"Okay. Pound the four corners into the ground. Not too far, though. Just a couple of inches."

Travis began to pound one of them in. "Like this?" he asked.

"Yeah. Looks about right. Do them all. Then drive a line of stakes for the wall ropes on the outside.

"Yup. I'll be done in the blink of an eye!" Travis said in a witty manner.

He began pounding the first row into the ground, working fast and furiously. He wanted to get all of the work done quickly so that they might scout around for elk before it got dark. If they knew where some were, they could probably get one first thing in the morning. He pounded on the stakes as hard and as fast as he could. The row wasn't very straight, but it was probably good enough. Surely his father would notice that the row was crooked, but that didn't matter now. He just wanted to get done and kept pounding away.

Even working at this pace, Travis could daydream. How grand it would be when they pulled into town with the elk in the back of the pickup! Surely they would stop at the coffee shop on Main Street, parking directly in front of the big glass windows for all to see. The huge antlers would be spread as wide as the pickup bed and rising up higher than the cab. It would be a record book seven by seven—seven points on each side of the antlers! All who walked by would ooh and ahh, being impressed by the hunting skill of Driskoll and his youngest son. Even the old-timers drinking coffee and playing cards would halt their game of Smear to admire the spectacular animal. They would all tell the pair how great an animal it was. Compliments and congratulations would abound. They would ask which area and drainage the elk was killed in, but the pair would only answer, "Up around Jackson." This was not a lie and it was a lot better than saying, "None of your business." Travis knew that a hunter never gave away his own hunting ground. It was kind of one of those laws of the land that they lived by. So many people would be complimenting and congratulating him that he would barely have time to eat his breakfast. Heck, the newspaper would probably show up and take their picture. They would probably even be in the hunting magazines as soon as those people heard about their elk!

Travis was finishing up pounding the stakes when an annoying thought came to him. What was his father doing? What could possibly be taking him so long to finish inside the tent? "If he'd hurry a little we could get to scouting. What's he doin'? Takin' a nap?"

Travis was surprised when he stuck his head into the tent and saw that the stove was set up and all of the gear that could be put inside was already in. He had been so busy working and daydreaming that he hadn't even noticed the twenty trips his dad must have made hauling the gear.

"Did you get 'em done?" his dad asked.

"Yeah."

"Are they straight?"

"Pretty much." Travis left it at that. He knew his dad wouldn't have even asked if he hadn't seen them and noticed that they weren't. Travis figured it was the contractor in Dad that made him notice things like that.

"All we've got left to do is to get our food and the horses' feed up in a tree and cut wood. Oh, yeah, water too," Dad said.

The two were headed out back to once again hoist the food and feed into a tree when Travis noticed for the first time that they were in an existing campground. Right there in front of his eyes was a small shelter made of pine limbs, with a fire pit right in front of it. The pit was grown full of grass but, once he looked at it, there was no doubt about what it was.

Travis's first thought was that maybe they had stumbled onto a mountain man's shelter a hundred, maybe even two hundred, years old. Maybe, just maybe, it was John Colter's mountain home. After all, being that old, most of it may have rotted by now. Travis knew Colter had explored most of this area. Wouldn't this make a story to tell Hal!"

He couldn't hold back his excitement at the thought. "Dad! You see that? Someone else has been camped here." He rambled on, not giving his dad a chance to respond. "Suppose it was Colter? Coulda been. I bet it was!"

His dad laughed and said, "No, Bud. I don't reckon it was Colter or Jackson or Bridger, or any of the others. I think it was the Driskolls."

Travis gave him that blank look that a person gives when he doesn't know what another is talking about.

"It's our camp," his dad explained. "We've been camping in this spot for eighteen years now."

"You camp in the same spot? Always?"

"Yeah."

"Why?"

"Well, I guess because it's convenient and comfortable."

"Oh," Travis said, still acting a bit stunned.

"Well, Bud, I guess it's like a pair of boots. Once you've worn them for a long time, they're comfortable. A lot more so than the hard new ones that make blisters. You never get rid of old boots 'til they're so worn out that they're no good anymore."

"I guess."

"Well, no one has ever been here when I got here, so this is like my parking spot in the mountains. C'mon, let's get this stuff up in the air. Got somethin' else I want to show ya."

The two came to a meat pole and hoisted the food up into the air, then retrieved the feed and did the same.

Travis had met the idea of camping in the same spot for years with disappointment, but now he began to see some advantages. It was work that he was thinking about. Number one, they didn't have to build a meat pole tall enough to hang the food and supplies out of the reach of bears, which would have meant a minimum of two hours' work. Second, there was a shelter and a fire pit, another couple of hours. Travis thought maybe it was not at all bad. Maybe it was good.

The feed and food were hoisted and Matt said, "C'mon. I'll show ya."

Travis didn't know what, but he followed. They came to a tree by the shelter and his dad pointed. There, on the trunk of a huge pine tree, were carved the names of his dad and his two brothers. The carving was almost artistic. Travis could tell that each of the three had carved his own name into the tree. The names circled around the tree. The oldest carving, of course, was Matt, their father. Then there were the carvings of his two brothers, Scott and Jess.

Scott was Travis's oldest brother. He was married now, and working in Chicago for an airline company. He didn't hunt much anymore. As Dad said, "It just doesn't interest Scott these days and that's okay, because it takes all kinds to make a world. Scott is a good person and a good family man, and that's most important."

Now, Jess. Well, Jess was Travis's hero. He was quite possibly the best hunter and greatest outdoorsman who had ever lived. He was off to the University for his second year of college, studying to be a veterinarian. Jess loved animals, especially horses. He could get a horse to go anywhere or do anything. He was amazing! It wasn't only Travis who thought so. Everybody in town did. When it came time to go hunting, if the opportunity arose to go with Jess Driskoll, you went. He had the uncanny ability to find animals even when no one else could. Travis had heard people say that the next time they went hunting with Jess, they were going to ride in his hip pocket so they wouldn't miss any of the action. Yeah, Jess was a legend around town and now, after seeing the carving, Travis wished that his brother were here.

He wasn't, though. He couldn't take a whole two weeks off from college to hunt. At least, that's what he said. These days, Jess hunted the Snowy Range near the University on weekends. He had told Travis that the elk weren't as big there, but there were quite a few of them.

"You'll have to carve your name in the trunk," his dad said.

"Yeah. Right beside Jess's name!"

His dad smiled and said, "Yeah, right beside Jess." He knew how much Travis loved and idolized his brother and it warmed his heart to think about it.

"You can carve your name tomorrow. We still have things to do tonight. C'mon."

CHAPTER 9

The firewood was piled up and that left only to get a couple of jugs of water and their camp would be ready for mountain living. Dad was filling a jug with water when he noticed Travis picking something up off the ground. "What did ya find?" he asked.

"Oh, just an old rifle casing."

"Oh?"

"Yeah. It's a 30-06."

"Hmmm. Maybe, just maybe, Colter dropped it right there! Yep. It was probably Colter's."

Travis looked down at his father and said, "Probably," in a tone just as wise as his father had used.

"Better look around," his father joked. "Maybe you'll find one Bridger left."

Travis didn't say anything. He knew he could not win this battle of the minds. He also knew that this would be ongoing for at least a while. His father would lay it on him every chance he got.

It was approaching that mountain dark now that Travis had learned about the night before. In about an hour the two would be confined to the tent because of the darkness. As they headed up the trail with the water, Dad could not pass up the opportunity. "Look, Bud! Over by the bush."

Travis looked, but he couldn't see anything.

"No. Look there. It's an elk skin jacket. I bet it's Colter's!" Dad roared with laughter. When he saw Travis's long face he said, "I'm sorry, Bud. I'll try not to hack on you so bad. But it is fun." He was still half chuckling.

"It's okay," Travis said. "I'll get ya back, guaranteed!"

Immediately after the words were out of his mouth, Travis realized that it was a mistake. What had he done? His father had said he would lay off, but instead of just accepting the apology and dropping the matter, Travis had confronted him with a challenge. Now it was war, and he knew Dad would really lay it on him.

Travis sat outside of the tent and thought about what he could do to get even with his father for teasing him, but he couldn't come up with anything.

It was about half dark now and his mind once again drifted off to elk. He wondered if there were any elk, especially big bulls, nearby. As he stared across the meadow, at least part of his question was answered. A group of cow elk began to appear out of the dense black timber. Travis didn't move. He didn't say a word. He just sat and watched. Within a minute there were eleven head standing with their faces down, grazing and working their way across the meadow to the spring where Travis had watered the horses. It was getting darker, and now Travis could only see their outlines in the fading light. He thought he could make out horns on one of the heads. Probably a spike.

Finally he stood up and howled like a coyote. The elk bolted and ran off, but only as far as a little knoll at the edge of the meadow. Once on the knoll, they turned around, stood still and looked for him. There was just enough lingering light so that the knoll silhouetted them and Travis could make out their faint outlines. Then one of the elk barked at him. Not once, but twice! Travis had never heard this sound before. It was a noise somewhere between the sound of a dog's bark and a crow's call.

Dad had heard Travis howl and stuck his head out the tent door. "What ya doin'?" he asked.

"Oh, just scarin' the elk," Travis replied. "They were right here by the water."

"They were, huh?"

"Yeah. One of 'em barked at me kind of like a dog."

"Where they at now?"

"Gone. Gone into the timber again."

"Well, good. Ya better get in here and eat."

Travis went into the tent and found that his father had cooked up some dinner for them. It wasn't a fancy meal, but they hadn't eaten anything except some dried fruit, nuts and seeds since breakfast. To-night they would have a hearty meal of instant mashed potatoes, gravy, biscuits, corn, and hamburgers. Travis was famished. He couldn't ever remember eating so much. His dad had cooked enough for four but, between the two of them, they ate it all.

Travis cleaned his plate, set it down, and started digging for the licorice. They both loved licorice and there was a mutual understand-ing between them that it would be their dessert for each meal. After all, they had brought twenty bags of it with them and they agreed there was no sense in having to haul half of it back.

They had each had a couple of pieces of licorice and were lying back on their sleeping bags when Matt said, "Don't even think about going to sleep yet. I believe you have some homework to do."

This was the first time Travis had thought about that. Not only had he not thought about it, but he had also forgotten the pencil and paper. What was he gonna tell his dad? He couldn't think of an excuse, so he said, "I don't have much to do. I can get it in a day or so." He must have really sounded pathetic with his attempt at an excuse.

"Did you forget something?" his dad questioned.

"Well . . ."

"Don't worry. I got ya covered." Dad handed Travis a spiral note-book and pencil. "Don't worry a bit, Son. I had Colter drop these by while I was cookin' dinner." He laughed and went on, "Do a good job. And don't forget to write about yesterday," he reminded Travis as he doubled up his pillow under his head to get more relaxed.

"I will," Travis said with a forced, almost scowling, smile. This Colter stuff was really getting old.

Travis began writing, moving the lantern each time he moved or rolled over to get the best light possible. He wrote about everything that had happened in the two days since they left the house. He even wrote about the mountain man, John Colter. It was homework. It wasn't fun, yet it wasn't terribly disgusting either. In no time at all he had written four pages and figured if he did one more he'd probably be overdoing it. He didn't write on front and back of the paper, and he knew why. There were seventy sheets of paper in the notebook and, if he wrote big and only on one side , he could spend more time doing fun things. Yes, it would appear as though he had put endless hours of work into his journal. Mrs. Goodman was much easier to fool than his dad, and Travis knew that this approach was one that would work!

When he was done with that fifth page, he closed the notebook and stashed it up in the corner of the tent by his pillow. "What time we leaving in the morning?" he asked.

"I figure about three. Yeah, three would be good," his dad replied as he heated water on the stove.

"Why three?"

"Well," Dad paused, "by the time we get rollin' in the morning, it'll be four, four-thirty maybe."

"It doesn't get light until six-thirty or so," Travis said, inviting an answer.

"If we get out early, we can probably locate elk somewhere in the valley by listening for them to bugle. Think about it, Bud. When did you hear the elk bugle last night?"

"I don't know. But it was dark out."

"Yeah, it was dark. The rut's all but over now, and that's about the only time of day you're gonna hear them bugle."

The conversation went on for a few more minutes and Travis was handed a wash rag and a tub of water. "Wash and get ready for bed. Three o'clock comes early and you'll need your beauty sleep for tomorrow!"

Travis took the rag, washed up, and started getting ready for bed. He procrastinated for a few minutes, getting his clothes and boots out for in the morning. Finally he could sense that his dad was getting impatient, and he crawled into his sleeping bag. The bag was cold when he crawled in, and Travis thought about crawling out and sleeping on top of it because the tent air was very warm. Deciding to stay in it, however, was the right decision. Within seconds his body heat had warmed the flannel type cloth inside the bag, and he knew he would be warm all night. Even if the fire in the stove went out, he had read that his bag was good for twenty degrees below zero. He felt warm, safe, lonely, and anxious all at the same time. There were only Travis and his father. They were truly alone.

CHAPTER 10

Travis's dreams that night were a jumble. He dreamt about elk some, but the anticipation of hunting with his father the next day kept him from resting for very long periods at a time. Unlike the nights before, he could not remember the dreams and, each time he tried, he couldn't tell if he had been sleeping or dreaming while he was awake.

One dream he did remember, though, was about John Colter, the mountain man who had explored this country, even this valley, over 150 years ago. Travis had written a report about Colter in the fourth grade. He remembered that there were legends about the mountain man escaping the Indians and wandering into Yellowstone Park. Colter was probably the first white man to see the geysers and mud pots. Legend says that he thought he had found Hell. But Travis's dream associated the man with survival somehow. In the dream, Colter was squatting in the lodge pine shelter at the edge of their camp, huddled up to a small fire, fighting off the deep snow and winter's cold.

When the dream left him, Travis was wide awake and wondering about what it had meant. He finally figured out that it meant he was tired of being razzed about Colter, the shelter, and the rifle casing.

The boy could no longer sleep and, once again, had no idea what time it was. Anxiety and nervousness had overtaken him again. He didn't want to leave at three or four in the morning when it was pitch black outside. It would be better to wait until daylight, he thought. After all, what if they ran into elk in the dark? They wouldn't even be able to see one to shoot it.

The real truth, though, was that Travis had a slight fear of the darkness and the unseen. Rationalizing and thinking about the fear didn't seem to help. It only made him more nervous. He wondered what he was scared of, or why he was scared. He didn't know. But he did figure out that he was more scared of the dark before the light and less scared of the dark after the light. This realization totally confused him. Morning or night? What did it really matter?

Was his father scared of the dark, Travis wondered, feeling suddenly cooler air on his face, ears, and neck. He slid his body back down into the bag for warmth and pondered this. Maybe all people are scared of the dark and they just don't want to admit it. This was a very intimidating place, with the bears, mountain lions, and other wild animals mostly hiding in the daytime and lurking out of the evil dark timber at night to prey on whatever they could find. Heck, maybe there were even ghosts and spirits out there waiting to seize the moment for disaster! He didn't know about these things either, but he was scaring himself thinking about them, so he would try not to think about them anymore.

He decided he would follow his father and that he wouldn't mention anything about being scared. After all of the razzing he had taken about Colter, he was going to try to be real careful about what he said for the remainder of the trip.

Not thinking about the lurking darkness proved to be a tough task. But Travis did try!

CHAPTER 11

The huge six point bull stood on the rise near the creek, admiring the harem of fourteen cows and calves that he had managed to keep for the entire mating season. He was feeling exhausted this cold breezy autumn morning, and was nearly one hundred pounds lighter than he had been a short month ago.

He had not eaten much the previous night, as he had not eaten much in the previous weeks. His challengers ever near and ever present had kept him on guard day and night, always looking, watching, and lurking—waiting for the monarch to make a mistake. Then they would rush in and steal his harem or, at least, part of it.

The giant bull had reigned over his territory now for four years and had the battle scars to prove it. Several of his challengers were his own sons. They were not yet physically strong enough to actually challenge the old bull, but they acted as the constant antagonist, always there, lurking and keeping him on guard. They did not ever allow him a moment's rest. Working as a team, they were present twenty-four hours a day. They had the same paternal instincts as he to pass their genes on to the next generation. As of yet, however, they did not have the power to take a harem or, in most cases, even a single mate, much less the power to keep it once they had it.

He marched back and forth now on the rise, counting and checking his harem with nervous anticipation, constantly worried that one of his cows may try to escape or leave him or, even worse yet, be taken by one of his nearby rivals. The vigil was endless. He decided that he had better verify his dominance and began to thrash his head around, showing off the mighty antlers to the cows. Then, to warn challengers and would-be herd bulls, he threw his head back and bugled and grunted loudly into the dark of the night. He did this not once, but twice.

His bugle was not answered by any of the nearby bulls or spikes. It was answered only by another bull perhaps a mile away. The old bull wondered if this was another herd bull, or was this finally a bull large enough to be a threat to him. Maybe it was just a weakling far enough away to figure that he could get away with the threat. At the beginning of the rut, the old bull might have gathered his group and gone to see this opponent and show him who the king was. Now, though, he was tired and decided he would bugle one more time using his most intimidating voice. He had previously decided that, if the challenger answered and sounded like he was getting closer, he would quickly gather the harem and herd them in the opposite direction.

His shrieking bugle and grunt were answered. The answer came from only a few hundred yards away. The monarch's plan for escape was foiled by the unbelievably fast advance of the challenger. This night he would have to stay and fight. There was no time to retreat now and, if he did, it would have to be without his hard won and hard kept cows.

The challenger advanced, stopping fifty yards from the defender to show off and try to intimidate his foe into leaving the battlefield without a fight. His bugle and grunt combinations were equally intimidating, and his antlers and physical attributes were the equal of the defender's. Court side observers gathered to see the coming battle and to see if, during the heat of battle, they might steal a cow or two.

Both bulls would try to win by intimidation first, and only use actual physical battle as a last resort. For ten minutes they used their best antics to try to scare the other into leaving. The two constantly faced each other so as not to give the other an opening to charge an exposed body. The points on their antlers could be lethal if they were thrust into the defenseless part of the other's body. The shrill grunting and bugling went on non-stop now. Neither was able to intimidate the other. Suddenly one of the observers rushed out into the meadow and took his chances at stealing the harem. He was a respectably mature animal, but he was still not in the same class as the two fighters. The defender caught a glimpse of the raider and wheeled to defend his flank as the raider sneaked in. The raider saw him coming and immediately knew that his attempt had been premature.

Now the challenger saw an opening and thought that he would give stealing the harem a chance. He trotted around the cows, shoving his huge tines into them to let them know that he meant business and that they had better cooperate. The cows put up very little resistance and, within seconds, were headed in the direction in which he had pointed them.

The monarch, having run off the raider, turned to see the thief trying to leave the battlefield with what he considered his property. It angered him to the point of rabid ferocity to see the invader trying to pull off such a cowardly stunt. He wheeled and once again was on the attack. Only this time, there would be a battle! The invader could not get the harem out of there as he had planned. He would either have to run off now or turn and fight. He had sized up his opponent and had decided that he could probably defeat him.

With heads down the two met, crashing their antlers together and roaring into battle. It sounded like giant pine trees being thrashed together, both pushing with every ounce of strength that they had. With noses only inches apart and eyes locked on the opponent's, the two waged war like the prize fighters that they were. The monarch gained a bit of an advantage when his fifth point found flesh and buried itself about four inches into the challenger's shoulder. The pain was horrifying, and it was adrenaline which kept the challenger fighting. He battled on as though nothing had happened.

It was now well after daylight and, under normal conditions, the monarch would have had his harem off into the safety of the black timber. On this morning, the two gladiators battled on.

CHAPTER 12

The sound of his father's voice saying, "Are you awake over there?" somehow soothed some of Travis's fear, and when the lantern was lit, it was even better.

Travis crawled out of his bag and began to get dressed for the hunt. "Put about four layers on," his father called to him as he was getting dressed.

"What do ya mean?" Travis asked.

"I mean, put a long john shirt on, your red huntin' shirt, a hooded sweatshirt, and a vest. Ya understand?"

"Oh. Yeah."

"The stars are bright. It'll be cold at dawn and probably hot by mid-afternoon."

Travis understood now. He'd have plenty on to be warm, and he could remove one garment at a time as it warmed up. It seemed to him that there were getting to be too many things to remember when you went hunting.

The pair ate just fruit and cereal this morning. There was no time for cooking and cleaning, and Travis would rather have cold cereal any morning, anyway. It was just a habit he had developed over the years and, even when he was offered other types of breakfast, he would decline for cereal.

They each packed a day pack and a fanny pack. The day pack held lunch, extra gloves, rope, a saw, and a camera. The fanny pack was loaded with first aid and survival materials such as Sterno and matches. His dad had told him that, while you were camping in the mountains, you never, ever, left camp without the ability to build a fire! And Travis knew why. If he were to get lost or hurt, or if a storm were to set in, he would have the ability to keep from freezing. Most people who die in the mountains die of exposure. Travis had had a lot of lectures and lessons on survival, and he figured he could get by.

Skeeter and Annie would again be their mounts for the day, and would probably be their mounts every day for hunting. The other three horses would stay at camp and graze on the tall meadow grass.

It took only about twenty minutes to get the horses all watered, saddled, and ready to go. With rifles in the scabbards and the 44 on his hip, Dad said, "Mount up!" Travis didn't know how they would ever be able to tell where they were going, and he hoped the horses could see better than he could. His pupils had dilated and adjusted themselves as much as possible in the darkness, but he still could barely see.

Now he had to question it. "Why we leaving so early?" he asked.

"This is the time I always leave on opening day," his father replied.

"I know. But why?"

"Well, I guess it's a habit, but uhh, well, let's get goin'. I'll explain on the way."

Travis didn't know how they would get anywhere without being able to see, but he stuck his feet lightly into Annie's ribs to get her to follow Skeeter as his dad led the way.

"Okay. So tell me," Travis prompted.

"The bulls are at the end of the rut now, and they're still trying to keep their harems and fight off challengers. They're active and bugle at night, but once it gets daylight they will probably go quiet. Ya understand?" his father asked.

"I guess. But you can't shoot 'em at dark!"

"I know that, Bud. But you can locate the area they're in by listening for them to bugle. If you know where they are, you have a better chance of sneakin' up on them."

"Yeah, but you can't see 'em!"

Matt was growing tired of trying to explain it, but figured he would try one more time. "Okay. Let's say we slept until daylight and then left camp looking for elk. Remember I said elk very seldom bugle during the day this late in the year. Are you with me so far?"

"Yeah."

"Okay. So, if we leave late and don't hear any elk, we decide to hunt the north side of the hill across the creek because we think it looks like a good spot. We may find that there's elk in there, but we might also hunt all day over there and never see an elk or any sign of one. Still with me?"

"Uh huh."

"So by leaving early, we'll know which hill has elk by listening. Understand?"

"Yeah. I guess so," Travis replied in a not too convincing tone.

"Well, just stay with me. You'll understand in a bit," his father assured him.

"It's not very cold out, is it, Dad?"

"No. But it will be when it starts to get light."

"Where we headed?" Travis asked. He found that the small talk kept his mind off the fact that it was very dark out and even eerie when they rode by a tall pine area. It was pitch black and there were shadows wherever the trees grew near the trail. "How could this be?" he wondered to himself.

"I got this spot. It's a U-shaped park. It's like my honey hole, I guess. It's about a mile to the west of here," his father replied.

"Ever get an elk there, Dad?"

"No. But I've seen a monster bull there three years runnin' on opening day. If he's still hangin' there, we'll probably hear 'im!"

Travis didn't respond, and the two rode on in silence. He understood better now, but he wondered why his dad had not shot the bull in previous years. He concluded in his mind that his dad had probably just not gotten close enough to the big bull. Travis hoped that they would find the bull on this morning. It would probably even be larger than it was last year.

They had ridden for what Travis guessed to be about a half mile when they came to a huge bend in the trail. Travis couldn't see it now, but they had actually crossed over the top of the hill behind camp and were now on its south slope. There were fewer trees here, and the breeze had picked up considerably. It was actually quite cool now, and Travis pulled the hood on his sweatshirt up over his ears. He tied the hood down as tight as he could, hoping to cut off the wind and keep it from reaching his neck.

Suddenly his father stopped Skeeter in front of him and said, "Did ya hear that?"

Travis hadn't, and probably wouldn't with the hood tied over his ears. He rode Annie up beside Skeeter and said, "What?"

"Take that hood off," his father commanded.

"Why?"

"So you can hear. That's why!" Dad answered in a sharp, deliberate manner.

Travis didn't really want to pull the hood down, but he did as his father told him. He pulled it down and listened carefully. All he could hear was the breeze in the tops of the trees. Suddenly he did hear something! It was not really clear and it was at least a half mile below them. He was sure that it was an elk bugling. He pointed to a spot below them and said, "Down there!"

"Yeah, he's there," Matt said, "and I think that he's in the U-shaped park. We can ride down here a ways and then we'll have to walk."

The sun still could not be seen as the two rode down the winding switch back trail, but Travis knew it would be coming up soon, as the sky was beginning to lighten a little. The trail that they were on was steep, and several times Annie was on her haunches sliding a bit more than walking. Travis was very happy he could see a little now! His mind kept floating from elk, especially the big bull, to riding Annie. It required a lot of his attention because of the steepness of the trail.

They were just about down to what appeared to be a flatter area when they heard the bull bugle. The sound of the elk bugling made the hair on Travis's neck stand on end. He was close. Really close. But Travis couldn't see him anywhere. The bull was either in the timber or just far enough away that he couldn't be seen in the morning's predawn glow. Travis wished that it were daylight. He thought that they probably could have gotten this bull if it were light enough. Anticipation and excitement had taken over. There was no fear in Travis now—only high expectations!

Just as they reached the flat part of this hill, another bull bugled. Travis wondered, "Was it the same one?" He barely had time to ponder this when he heard another bugle, then another, and without hesitation, another. Travis thought it sounded like two different voices, but he wasn't sure.

Then Dad said it. "Sounds like two different bulls. Maybe even more! Better get down there. I think they're in my meadow."

They tied the horses up at the edge of the timber, a few yards off the trail. Then they grabbed a fanny pack, backpack, and the 300 mag and headed down the trail. Travis thought they should be moving faster than they were, and practically ran his father over as they were going down the hill. He didn't want the elk to leave and, as slow as they were moving, he figured they may be gone before the pair of hunters got there.

The sky was completely blue now and, even in the dark timber, a man could see well enough to make out animals. The cross hairs of a scope could easily find the rib cage of an elk in an open meadow. Travis's heart was pounding, not from being tired, but rather from the sheer expectations of the moment. He was sure the elk could hear his racing heart, but he could do nothing to slow it down. The bugling continued. It was now closer than ever—no more than 150, maybe 200 yards away.

Now Matt slowed down to a slow walk, watching all around him. He turned around and said, "Shhh!" then whispered in Travis's ear. "We're really close. Gotta be quiet. Real quiet." With his finger in front of his mouth giving Travis the hush sign, he proceeded to the edge of the meadow.

It seemed to Travis that there was not a square inch of earth on the forest floor that was not covered with crunchy branches or snapping twigs. It was impossible to be quiet. As the two pressed forward, Travis noticed a fallen tree that would give them the needed cover to scan the meadow.

They edged their way up to the log and knelt down hiding behind it. It was light now, and they knew that the elk were close. They scanned the meadow from the vantage point, but the elk were nowhere to be found. They looked more carefully, but there were no elk to be seen. "How could this be?" Travis wondered. He knew they were in this park. Suddenly a loud shrieking bugle confirmed his thoughts. Then came the sound of antlers locked together in battle. The sound came from their right, just over a small rise in the meadow. On their hands and knees, they moved toward the sound ever so slowly. Staying at the edge of the timber and using it as cover, the two hunters were able to sneak up on the two bull elk locked up in a bitter fight.

They nestled down in behind a small bunch of pine seedlings and watched.

CHAPTER 13

Both bulls were huge, mature herd bulls. One was a heavy beamed six by six and the other an equally heavy six by seven. Both would be trophy bulls for any hunter. Travis watched in awe. Even his vivid imagination did not do these animals justice. They were larger and more beautiful than he had ever dreamed. The huge tan and buff bodies with dark manes only 30 yards away kept his eyes and mind working. He wondered what they were fighting for. Of course, he finally realized, it was over a harem. What else could it be?

He wondered which one would win. At this point, it looked as though they were equally strong and equally skilled. The only possible advantage Travis could see that either animal had was that one extra point on the six by seven bull.

The two bulls pushed on, neither one gaining and neither giving. At times they would push with the power of a bulldozer, and at other times it came to a halt and they loosely mashed their horns together, not leaving or turning but perhaps resting, Travis thought.

It was after one of these intermissions that an event occurred that Travis thought would change the tide of the battle. On the initial thrust, the six by six twisted his rack skillfully and buried a tine into the six by seven's shoulder. The tine stayed buried for five to ten seconds and, when it came loose, it ripped muscle and hide as blood began to spew. Travis winced. The old bull did not seem to feel any pain, though, and the battle raged on—hooves digging, antlers crashing, and dust flying.

Suddenly Travis wondered which one his dad was going to shoot. He thought probably the six by seven. But when he turned to look, he was shocked to find his father videotaping the fight. Then he thought, "He'll probably wait 'til the fight's over and shoot the winner."

The bulls fought on for several more minutes, but it was obvious the wounded bull was wearing down. It seemed to Travis that soon the six by seven would turn and flee, leaving the six by six as their trophy. The fight didn't end, though. The six by six would not relent long enough for the wounded bull to retreat. "Are they going to fight to the death?" Travis wondered. His dad had told him that only on very rare occasions would two bulls fight to the end. It appeared as though this may be one of those times. The wounded bull was wanting to leave, but to turn and attempt a retreat would leave his ribs and abdominal area exposed for a split second. That would be all the time his foe would need to once again run a tine into him. And in those vulnerable areas, it would be fatal!

Travis now watched in terror. He wanted it to stop. In his twelve and a half years, he had never witnessed anything so brutal. What had begun as a majestic fight had turned into a grueling ugly mismatch.

Finally the wounded bull could not push anymore. His survival now depended on finding a quick escape. During one of the mini breaks, he pulled his antlers free and turned to run. The winner, though, was too quick and thrust an antler into the fleeing bull's ribs. Travis could not stand it anymore. He jumped up and yelled and screamed the loudest piercing scream he had. "Stop it! Stop it!" he screamed. "Stop!"

The victor paused for a split second to see the intruder, looking just long enough for the loser to escape into the timber. Now Travis wondered if he had been too late in breaking up the fight. Had the tine into the rib cage connected with a vital organ? Would the bull live?

By now, both bulls were gone and Travis heard his father say, "You okay?"

Travis looked up at him and said, "Yeah. Why didn't you shoot one?"

"I don't know."

"Why?" Travis repeated.

"It just didn't seem fair. They were fighting and had no idea. It just wasn't right!"

Now Travis had recovered from the shock of the fight and didn't want to let on that he had felt bad about the one bull almost killing the other. He chewed off the bottom end of a grass stem and said, "I'd have shot the six by seven."

CHAPTER 14

Travis and his dad sat in this spot for a while after the elk left. They were reminiscing and discussing the fight and whether or not Travis's yelling had anything to do with the bull's narrow escape. They both agreed that it had, and they each hoped the wounded animal would recover.

"He'll probably just lay low and heal for now, then head for the refuge to winter," Matt said. He was referring to the National Elk Refuge in Jackson, where thousands of elk winter each year.

"I can't believe it. They were gonna kill each other," Travis remarked. "It's unbelievable!"

"Son, I know you're disappointed that I didn't shoot an elk. But look at the positive. What you just saw, most people only ever dream of seeing. That's including even professional hunters and outfitters. Most of them have never seen a fight like this and, if they did, no one would believe them."

Then Travis remembered that they had it on tape. "Proof!" he thought.

"Heck, Trav, a lotta people never even see an elk when they go out huntin'. Besides that, the kill is only a part of the experience of hunting."

"What's that?" Travis asked. Now he knew he was going to get an earful.

"Hmmm," his father smiled. Then he began to speak. "Hunting is a different experience for everyone. For me, it's like building a oneness with nature. I don't know how to explain it, other than to say it's the *experience* I'm after, not just the kill. Hunting isn't just killing. It's more.

56

It's an experience with nature. Over the years, I've killed elk, and some pretty good bulls at that. But now I just don't have the taste for it. I don't think there's anything wrong with it, though. I just don't have to reaffirm myself right now."

He could see that Travis was a bit confused about all of this and he decided to lighten matters up again. "Heck, the meat on one of those old bulls would scare off a hungry dog. Besides that, Colter told me to shoot a yearling cow if we were gonna hang it in his camp!"

Travis smiled and told his dad he was off the hook for now.

"Since I'm off the hook, let's go see if Skeeter and Annie are still around."

They gathered their things and made their way back through the timber.

The pair spent the rest of the morning riding ridge trails above their camp and, for the first time since they had arrived at the trailhead, Travis saw the beauty of the country that he was hunting in. The tall peaks and lush valleys were complemented by green pine, golden aspen, and practically every other color known to man. He figured he must be awfully close to heaven, as good as he felt after just missing getting the elk of a lifetime. All this time, he had thought his dad was just in a dry spell when it came to elk. Now he wondered how many bulls had been allowed to escape over the years.

The mountain air had warmed to the point where Travis wore only the shirts now and, as he tied his sweatshirt to the saddle horn, he thought about how cold it had been earlier, and how he, himself, had been chilled before they heard the elk bugling. After the elk started to bugle, he could not remember being cold. He had been too involved to even notice he was cold. "Amazing!" he thought.

He also wondered if they might see the bulls again and, if they did, whether his dad might reconsider and shoot one of them. Even though they had the proof on tape, Travis wanted the trophy in the worst way. In a way, though, he did feel a little better about the events of the morning. He had worked every day, never shrugging off work, always doing what he was told, and never pouting or scowling about it. He had truly heeded his mother's advice. To top that off, his dad knew how badly he wanted to get a big bull on this, his first hunt. As far as

Travis was concerned, Dad should have done it, if for no other reason, just for him!"

Now Travis thought to himself, "I'm done whining and feeling sorry for myself." He really kind of understood what his father had said and probably respected it more than his father knew.

CHAPTER 15

The two hunters were now riding down a draw through some heavy pine timber on a wide game trail. The trail was heavily used, Travis could tell, because of the width of the trail, the amount of deer and elk droppings near it, and the looseness of the dirt wherever the trail turned. The twigs and branches were all ground up from hooves pounding on them. When they were out of the timber, Travis was surprised to see their tent and horses. He had not realized where they were, but now he assessed that they had spent most of the morning riding the mountain right behind camp. He also thought that the trail they came out on was probably the one that the elk which had come for water the night before had used.

They rode straight to the spring and dismounted as the horses began to drink. The smell of horse sweat was abundant as Travis threw his stirrup up over the saddle. He could feel the heat radiating off Annie's body as he loosened the cinch. Travis thought he really felt at ease and relaxed, especially considering his surroundings on this day. He was, at least, as relaxed as a boy his age could be this far out in the wilderness.

When the horses had finished drinking, Travis and his dad pulled the saddles off them and picketed them so they could eat and rest.

Travis's mind jumped to the tree and the name which needed to be carved into its bark. That was his own name, of course, and as he headed for the tree on a run his father called, "What ya gonna do?"

"Carve my name," Travis replied.

"Sure. Go. Leave me alone to fix lunch. See how ya are?"

Travis knew his dad was just joshin' him, and he reached into his pocket to find his knife as he ran. When he got to the tree, he looked up and confirmed what he had seen the night before. He figured it would take him three or four hours to carve his name in as nice as Jess had, but it would be time well spent. After all, what would four hours be in the ten days they had left to be here in camp?

Travis thought the tree was like a monument—a monument not so unlike monuments in places like Washington, D.C. People stopped in Washington to look at monuments. He was sure of this, even though he had never been there. Anyhow, if he were in Washington, that's what he would do. Thus, he reasoned, people would probably stop here and look at the monument and give his father, brothers, and himself recognition. He imagined that someday it would be an elk hunter's dream to see the famous *Driskoll Elk Hunting Monument*. Therefore, he would do a very fine job of carving.

Travis looked around for something to stand on so he could reach the spot where the carving was. It wasn't real high up in the tree, but it was up high enough that it would be hard for him to work on without some sort of stool. He looked near the edge of the timber for fifty yards on either side of camp, but came up with nothing. The only stump he could find weighed much more than he could carry. He thought about all of the gear they had brought along, but there was nothing there to use, either. He wished he had a ladder.

Then it hit him. A ladder! He would make one. He ran to the tent and got a saw and a piece of the thin nylon rope. Next he searched for a couple of dead pine seedlings about two inches in diameter and began cutting. He pushed the saw back and forth across the base of the dead tree until he finally had it cut about two-thirds of the way through. Then he pulled on the tree with all of his might until it finally gave away and broke. Deciding that sawing was taking too long, he ran back to the tent and grabbed an axe. The second tree went much faster. After both trees were down, he used the axe and saw to clean the limbs off the fallen trees. The trees were both about ten feet long and would make perfect ladder legs. Travis decided to cut about two feet off each end and again cut each of those pieces in half. These smaller pieces would be used for the ladder steps. Four steps would be plenty, he thought. After all, he only needed to get about two foot up into the air and he could reach the height he wanted to reach.

Travis thought his plan was coming together brilliantly when his father called, "Lunch is on!"

Travis didn't really want to stop work on his creation, but his stomach told him he was hungry, so he headed for the tent. The aroma of bacon filled the air as he entered, and the tent seemed dark and not as friendly as it had felt the night before.

"Ya get to carvin' yet?" Matt asked.

"No."

"What ya been doin?"

"I'm building a ladder so I can reach," Travis replied, looking for approval.

"Oh. Jess and Scott just led old Buck up there and sat on his back while they did theirs."

"I never thought of that."

"Well, a ladder's good though, ya know. When you're done, we'll leave it for Colter," Matt said with a big grin on his face.

Travis decided he could be a wise guy, too, and countered, "Yeah. Maybe if old Colter had a ladder, he could see them Blackfoot comin' a little sooner!"

"Yeah," his father laughed. "I'll help ya and we'll build the deluxe model, just for him."

After polishing off the bacon and soup, the two went right to work on the ladder. They figured the dishes could wait until dark. Travis was amazed at how much faster his father could notch the pine poles with the axe than he could. In no time at all, he had four notches in the poles and Travis began tying the cross pieces on, making a nice ladder to reach with.

As the last knots were tied, he picked the ladder up from the ground and leaned it up against the tree. It was perfect! The second step put him at just the right height to work on the carving.

Now, again, he dug out his knife and was ready to go to work when his father said, "If we're gonna make an afternoon hunt, we had better get goin'."

Travis wanted to get started with the carving, but it wasn't as though someone else was gonna take his spot. He jumped down and headed over to Annie to saddle her up.

CHAPTER 16

The two spent the afternoon riding the trails, always looking for elk sign or movement, but they had very little success. Travis wondered how a place which held so many elk in the morning could be so barren of the creatures in the afternoon. The elk had vanished like shadows at high noon in the middle of summer. They rode in and out of timber, through meadows, up and down hills for several hours, but no sign of elk.

"Where'd they go?" Travis asked his father.

"They're here. Probably just timbered up for the afternoon. They'll start movin' before dark."

They rode on, stopping only to glass a mountain side once in a while. But the elk would remain invisible this autumn afternoon.

As evening grew nearer, Travis noticed that they were not heading toward camp. This worried him a bit. Not only would they have to ride in the dark again, but how would they find their way?

"We headin' back?" he asked.

"Yeah," his father answered. But maybe we ought to watch a meadow down here just above the main trail 'til dark."

Travis wasn't crazy about this idea but, once again, he didn't say anything about not wanting to ride in the dark. He just followed.

The elk didn't show in this meadow either and, by the time they left, it was officially dark. At first Travis could see a little, but as they came off the hillside they had been on and hit the main trail, it grew even darker. It was dark almost to the point that he could not see Skeeter and Dad in front of him.

Suddenly Travis felt the urge to talk if, for no other reason, to make sure his father was actually there in front of him. "Sure is dark," he said.

"Yeah, it is," his father replied.

"How far are we from camp?"

"Only a couple of miles."

Travis figured a couple of miles wasn't too bad. But he wished secretly for a moon.

Matt continued on, telling Travis about a time he had spotted some elk on a mountainside about an hour before dark. He had sneaked up on them but couldn't find a bull in the group. The area he had been in was full of cliffs and drop offs, and he had no flashlight. When he realized that it was getting dark fast, he left the elk only feet away from him and headed downhill as fast as he could travel. The mountain he was on was steep and tough to go up or down, even in the daylight. He hadn't made it but about a third of the way down before it was pitch black out. "It was so black I couldn't see my hand in front of my face," he said.

"How'd you get down?" Travis asked.

"Well, I felt every step forward with my foot before I actually stepped. I got lucky. When I hit the bench above the creek, I tried to walk at a normal pace. I tried, but it didn't work. I kept running into trees. So dark I couldn't see them. So I felt my way down to the creek bank to a log that straddled the creek. I crawled across it."

"Were you scared?"

"I don't know if I was scared, but I have to say I was concerned. Thoughts ran through my mind. What if I fall off a cliff, or trip and break a leg? Yeah. I guess in a sense I was scared. It was dark out—darker than I had ever seen it."

"How long did it take you to get out?" Travis asked.

"All total, about two hours. About an hour on the mountain and about an hour findin' the pickup after I crossed the creek. It was parked about 100 yards from the creek, but it was so dark I couldn't find it. Now I always have a light with me."

The story had done nothing to eliminate Travis's fears. It only made his imagination work even more. "What if we can't find camp?" he thought. Then he stuck his hand in front of his face to see if he could see it. When he realized that he could see his hand, he blurted out, "It was darker than it is now."

"Yes, it was. Much darker!" his father replied.

"No!"

"Yes!"

"I wouldn't want to see that," Travis said.

"Why? You scared of the dark?"

"No," was his short reply.

Travis would never admit to that. He would much rather keep this secret to himself and fight it each day on his own. And he certainly hoped that it would not be that dark while they were here on this trip!

They continued on for what seemed like hours to Travis. When they finally came to camp, he realized he was actually very tired. He wished that he could just crawl into his sleeping bag and go to sleep, but that was out of the question. There were horses to be watered, dishes to wash, and supper to make.

When the work was finally all done, he crawled into his bag and thought about the events of the day—but only for a few minutes. That was as long as it took for him to fall asleep.

CHAPTER 17

Travis dreamed this night. He dreamed about the two bulls and even more elk.

He also dreamed about Colter. He actually talked to him. Colter described what it was like when he first discovered Yellowstone, otherwise known as "Colter's Hell." Travis could not remember much about the dream when his father jabbed him and said, "Get up!"

Travis didn't want to wake up. He wanted to sleep. He was more tired than he could ever remember being. But rolling over and burying his head in a pillow was not going to cut it this morning . He heard his father say, "Come on. We're gonna be late if ya don't get out here."

Travis thought, "Late for what? To let another bull walk off?" He didn't say it and he didn't even really mean to think it, but he did. Perhaps it was his thought only because he was so tired.

After a couple more minutes of thinking, he decided to force himself up out of the warm sleeping bag into the cold morning air of the tent. The fire had burned out in the night and neither Travis nor Matt had had enough energy or ambition to crawl out of his warm sleeping bag and throw a log in the stove. It was so cold Travis could see his breath in the dim lantern light. He didn't waste any time getting his clothes on this morning.

"Come on!" Matt said again as he stuck his head inside the tent. "Grab some goodies. You can eat on the way. We're late!"

Now the excitement began to grow and Travis was ready to hit the trail. Annie was also ready and, once again, the foursome rode out into the darkness. The morning was exactly like the previous one, only Travis could tell that they were headed the same direction they had gone the day before. He felt much more secure now that he had an idea about where he was, and his expectations were high. Would they see the big bulls again? Or maybe even a whole herd of elk? They had not even come close to the spot where they had heard the first bull bugle the previous morning and it was already getting light. Now Travis wished he had gotten up and helped get the horses ready. He thought, if he had, they would be further up the trail by now and in a better position to hear the elk. The breeze seemed to be stiffer this morning and increased in speed with the rising of the sun. It was completely light when they crossed over the top and headed down the steep trail.

Yesterday Travis had listened to the treetops rustling in the morning breeze. Today they were bent over in a gusting, howling wind. He forgot about elk for a few minutes and thought only about getting down the hill out of the wind. It bit at his face, ran up his sleeves, and even penetrated through his pants, cooling his legs and knees. The fancy new bandana he had gotten for this trip and his hood didn't seem to help. The wind slipped by them and chilled his back. All he wanted to do was get down out of the wind.

As they worked their way down the winding trail, the wind seemed to let down and, as they neared the bottom, it almost seemed to quit. "Maybe it has quit," Travis thought, but as they approached the timber, he could hear that he had been wrong. On the ground, there seemed to be only a bit more than a breeze. But the tops of the pine trees told a different story. They waved hard and furiously, banging each other, creaking, cracking, and popping. It didn't sound like a safe place at all. He wondered how many trees would break or fall over before the wind was finished.

Travis thought his dad must be cold, too, when they came to a small draw completely out of the wind and he stopped, got off Skeeter and sat down on the ground. "Come on down," he said to Travis. But before the sentence got out of his mouth, Travis was dismounted and sitting beside him.

"You cold?" Travis asked.

"Yeah. It's nippy."

"What we gonna do?"

"I think we'll head down and, if we don't see anything, we'll take the bottom trail back to camp. If we do see something, we'll hunt!"

"Sounds good to me," Travis said. He was somewhat disappointed about not seeing or hearing any elk this morning, but getting back to the tent out of the wind with the warmth of the stove sounded awfully good to him, also.

"Where do you think the elk are?" Travis asked.

"They're probably holed up in the timber by now. We ain't gonna find 'em unless we get in there and step on 'em. I hope this old wind's not blowin' in a storm."

Travis hoped that, too. He had been as cold as he wanted to be, and could not see or feel any good thoughts about snow. As they rode down toward the main trail, he actually hoped that they wouldn't see any elk. Riding in and out of the piercing northwesterly wind, Travis thought about how he would sit in front of the heat duct in his room at home on days like this, and he almost wished he were there. Surely his mom would have some warm soup and hot chocolate ready for lunch. "But," he thought to himself, "quit whining. This is where I want to be." Besides, once they were back in camp and had the stove cranked up, he could rotate between sitting in the warm tent and carving on the monument. "Maybe I can get it all done today," he thought.

The ride to the main trail went as his father had predicted, and there were no elk to be found this fine windy morning. When they turned to head for camp, the wind was now on their backs. Travis thought this was much better than having it in their faces as they had most of the morning. Now, with his hood up and shoulders shrugged up, he felt no wind going down his neck.

The pace quickened. Rather than walking the horses back to camp, they trotted most of the way. It was almost as though the horses wanted to call it quits for the day as much as their riders did. This brought Travis to wonder if the horses were cold, too. Or did they just want to get back to eat and drink?

Once back in camp, they again took care of the horses and, as soon as they were finished, they headed for the tent. Travis crawled into his sleeping bag as his father started a fire in the stove. The tent was cold, but the wind didn't penetrate it. It flopped and snapped at the sides, but didn't penetrate through the heavy canvas.

Travis thought he would only stay in the sleeping bag until the stove warmed up. Then when he was warm, he would go out and work on the carving for a while. That plan lasted for only about three minutes, though, as that is how long it took him to fall asleep.

When he awoke, he saw that his father was sleeping, and the tent was warm and friendly now. Travis felt his cheeks and they were not cold anymore. After rummaging for some fruit and a candy bar, he headed outside to start carving. Once again, he dug the pocket knife out, only this time he began to work. The second step on the ladder put him at just the right height.

Travis had decided he would use a fancy printed letter rather than cursive. The others were all printed and, besides, it would be impossible, at least for him, to carve in cursive. He carefully drew the outline of a T in the bark and, when he had it just the size he wanted, he begin digging and slicing slowly with the blade of the knife. He carved through the bark and into the wood of the tree, only gouging outside of the outline twice.

It took about forty-five minutes to get the T the way he wanted it and, as he headed back for the tent to warm up, he turned around and admired his handiwork. "Not too bad for a first try," he thought.

As Travis pulled the tent flap open and stepped inside, his dad woke up and said, "What ya doin'?"

"Started carvin'," Travis replied.

"Oh. How'd it go?"

"Good. Got a T. It's still awful windy and cold out there."

"I think I'll gather some firewood. It's gonna be cold tonight. With this wind, heck, it might snow," Matt commented. "Oh, and while I'm doin' the firewood, you get your journal out and write."

"Aww . . . " Travis began to protest.

"No! None of that! You get it out and when you come in to warm up you can write. You forgot it yesterday. No sense in gettin' behind on it now, is there?"

"I guess not." Travis went to his corner of the tent and dug out the pencil and notebook. He sat for a long time pondering what to write.

It seemed as though it took forever to get started, but when he finally did, the words flowed to the paper as he rambled on. He wrote about the two bulls, the ladder, Colter, and the wind. When the journal was finished he headed back out to the monument tree to carve an R.

The R proved to be a much tougher task then the T had been. Travis was only about half finished when he decided it was time to go in and warm up again. As he crawled off his ladder and turned, he was startled by the sight of an unfamiliar horse and its rider coming toward him.

CHAPTER 18

The rider rode a huge bay horse and didn't say a word until he was only a couple of feet from Travis. "Where's your dad?" the stranger asked in a loud, demanding voice.

By now Travis could tell by the stranger's jacket and hat that he was a game warden. Travis stammered a bit and said, "I . . . I don't know. I'll find him!" He scanned the area along the timber around to the tent, but didn't see his father anywhere.

Meanwhile, the stranger had crawled off the huge horse and Travis was amazed at the man's size. "He must be seven feet tall!" Travis thought. The man was huge by any standards. Travis was groping for words and finally managed, "Maybe he's in . . ." and pointed at the tent. The rest of the words just wouldn't come out, the huge man was so intimidating.

"Okay," the stranger said with a half smile, half scowl on his face. He turned toward the tent, leading his horse right up to the entry flap. Travis wanted to say, "Just a minute and I'll get him," but he couldn't. He was frozen in place and didn't move. He just watched and wondered what this game warden wanted from his dad. They had done nothing wrong as far as he knew. "What's up?" he wondered.

The stranger stood directly in front of the opening staring back at Travis, knowing he was making the boy very nervous. Suddenly he hollered toward the tent, "Driskoll, this is the law! If you're in there, come out with your hands up!"

Travis couldn't believe it. They had done nothing wrong and he couldn't figure out what was going on. He wanted to say something.

He wanted to ask what was wrong, but words would not come out of his mouth. Now the stranger was looking even meaner and Travis thought, "What if he's not really a game warden? What if he's some crazy person on the loose meaning to hurt us?" All of this and he was still frozen in his foot tracks.

It was only a few seconds but, to Travis, it seemed like hours before his father called out, "We don't need any game wardens around here!"

"Oh, no!" Travis thought. "What's going to happen?" Why had his father sounded so belligerent toward the warden? Now Travis was unconsciously moving toward the tent, wondering what was going to happen next.

Suddenly the tent flap opened, and he could see a big smile on his father's face. "Has he gone insane?" Travis wondered. "This is too serious a matter to be smiling at a time like this! What . . . ?"

Then he saw the warden smile, too, as his father reached out and shook the huge man's hand. He said, "Hello, Smitty! What ya up to?"

"Well, right now I'm havin' some fun with your kid out here. Had him worried, I think."

Matt Driskoll smiled again and chuckled. Then he said, "Imagine that! Did you get him?"

"Yeah. He was worried," Smitty replied. "He was stammering and stuttering—couldn't say a word for a minute!"

"So unlike you!" Matt said sarcastically. The two men laughed and talked about it some more.

Travis wasn't laughing, though. He failed to see the humor in the situation. "What's so funny about scaring a kid half to death?" he thought to himself. "Coulda had a heart attack or something." Travis had that mad, scowling look on his face when his father looked down and noticed that he wasn't joining in the laughter.

"Come on, Trav. It was just a joke! Smile a bit and meet my old friend, Smitty, here. Best warden in the state!"

Travis forced a smile to his cheeks and faintly said, "Hi."

"Besides that, Colter's over there by your tree just laughin' up a storm, and ya don't wanta make him mad. Right?" his father said.

Now Travis was mad. Not only had Smitty gotten him, but now his father had jabbed him as well. "Besides that," he thought to himself, "he told me he'd lay off on this Colter stuff. How did he know, anyhow? Maybe this *was* Colter's camp! Maybe it wasn't just a joke!"

Travis secretly wished that Colter would show up. Then the two of them would do a little practical joking themselves. "Boy, we could really get them back, Colter and I. Yup, we could!" he thought.

"Come in, Smitty," Matt was saying. "I got a cup of coffee brewin'."

Travis didn't follow the two men into the tent. Instead, he stomped back to his tree to finish the R. He had been cold before the stranger showed up. But now he was mad and had forgotten about being cold. He carved furiously on the R, making several deep gouges outside his outline.

Finally the R was complete, and Travis was really cold now. He decided that he would have to go back to the tent. Not that he wanted to be around his dad or Smitty, but because it was the only place to go to get out of the wind and get warm.

As he stuck his head into the tent, both men quit talking for a moment. Then his father said, "Figured you'd be in pretty soon. Ya still mad?"

Travis was honest this time. "Just a little," he replied.

"Sorry, then, I guess."

Smitty said he was sorry also, and now Travis felt better. He sat down by the warm, almost glowing stove, sucking up all the heat he could. He had not realized how cold he was, and he was thankful his father had the fire going. "Such a simple thing to be thankful for!" he thought.

Now Smitty spoke. "How are you likin' it so far, Travis?"

"It's great. Really great! We saw some big ones yesterday," Travis replied boastfully.

"Yeah, I heard. Pretty exciting, huh?"

"Yeah," Travis replied. "But we didn't shoot one of 'em."

"Maybe next time," Smitty replied. "Maybe next time. Heck, I've never even seen a fight like that. Wish I'd a been there!"

"We got it on film," Travis replied, trying to validate the genuineness of the fight. Perhaps he was fearing the notion that Smitty may not have believed him.

"Oh, yeah. And I'm gonna watch it if you'll send me a copy when you get home."

This guy didn't seem so bad, Travis thought after talking to him for a few minutes. He wondered how his dad and this warden had met. "How'd you meet my dad, Smitty?" he asked. "Did you bust him doing something wrong, or what?" This brought smiles to both men's faces.

"Yeah. I mean, no," Smitty replied.

"Which?" Travis asked, waving his hand back and forth. "Yes or no?"

"No. Your dad had a little run-in with a bear a long time ago, and I had to check it out. That's when we met. We usually see each other every year up here. Kinda like mountain men gettin' together when they cross each other's grounds."

Travis had heard this story about the bear a hundred times. It was a good story, and now it seemed even more real since he had met the warden. "I know." Travis began to tell the story.

"Years ago, before I was born, my dad was guiding a bow hunter during the archery season. They were bugling, trying to call in a bull when, suddenly, a grizzly appeared about ten yards away!" Travis was really hamming it up now, growling and roaring as he talked. "Both my dad and the hunter turned to run. But, as Dad turned, he fell down. The bow hunter kept right on running. Running right over my dad and leaving a hiking boot track right in the middle of Dad's backpack."

"Yeah," Smitty said. But before he could say another word, Travis continued.

"My dad always said that he thought for sure that he was bear meat! But, right where he fell, there was a huge pine limb laying on the ground. He grabbed the limb and scrambled to his feet waving it, yelling and screaming at the bear. For some unknown reason, the bear dodged off into the timber and disappeared."

Travis always thought the funniest part of the story was when his father turned around to go back to camp, figuring the bow hunter was already there. Dad was shocked to see the man standing only ten yards away, trying to nock an arrow!"

Then his father, who had been listening, spoke. "Yeah. The only thing he was going to do with that arrow was hurt himself, he was shaking so bad. Unbelievable!"

Travis said, "I bet they both had to clean their shorts out after that one!"

Smitty and Travis both laughed, but Matt only smiled. He never laughed about that incident. Travis glanced over at his father and decided that he should change the subject. He looked at Smitty and asked, "What brings you up here on a cold, windy day like this?"

"Well, I'm up here for the season. But right now I'm out going to camps letting hunters know we've got a major storm comin' in."

"When?" Travis asked, not really wanting to know.

"Two, three days," Smitty said, shaking his head back and forth in a serious manner. "It could be a big one. I told your dad about it just before you came in."

Travis was disappointed, and it showed on his face. He didn't want to leave. There were too many things to do yet. He wanted to stay! There was the monument, he thought, and what about the elk? They hadn't gotten one yet. He mulled it over in his mind. "We can't go back," he thought. "We just can't!" Then he said it. "We're not leaving, are we?"

His father looked at him sternly with that "don't throw a fit while we have company" look and said, "Smitty says it's gonna get bad. I know you don't want to go, but if we get snowed in up here, we'll be in trouble for sure. We just can't take that chance."

"Can we hunt just one more day?" Travis begged. "Please. We know where the bulls are. We could give it one more try, couldn't we?" Travis pleaded the best he knew how.

Finally his father said, "Okay. We'll try it for a few hours in the morning. It's against my better judgment, but we'll do it."

Smitty finished one more cup of coffee, then said, "Thanks for the coffee, Matt. Gotta get movin'."

Matt smiled and said, "You're welcome to spend the night if you like."

"No, I gotta ride to the east and spread the word about the weather."

Travis joined in. "In the dark?" he questioned.

"Yeah. My old bay, he knows his way. He'll keep me goin' straight. Besides, I got a lot of ground to cover. I'd like to get out of here before the snow's too deep!"

"It's gonna be awful dark tonight, though," Travis persisted.

"Well, I'm not scared of the dark. If I get a move on it, I can make it to my patrol cabin by eight or nine o'clock."

Travis simply nodded. He didn't want Smitty to know he was afraid of the blackness of the night in these mountains, and to keep talking now would surely give himself away.

The three stood up simultaneously and Smitty led the way out of the tent. As he pulled himself up onto the huge bay horse, he said, "If you hunt tomorrow, at least make sure to get started out. Game and Fish flew Yellowstone yesterday and reported the elk are bunchin' up. There's one herd, they figure about a thousand head, just a couple miles north of here."

"Kind of early for that," Matt commented.

"Yeah, a month or so early," Smitty replied. "That's what's got me thinkin' this storm's gonna be a doozy! Them elk know a lot more about these things than men do. If they head for the refuge, you better be on their tails! I'll ride by here on my way back and make sure you're not still here."

"Thanks," said Matt, "but we'll be gone. You take the quickest route outta here. Oh, and take care of yourself!" he added.

"I will," Smitty replied. "And, Travis, don't worry about me in the dark. If I get lost, I'll stop and ask Colter for directions!" With a grin, he jabbed the bay gently in the ribs and was off.

Travis hollered behind him as he rode off, "You do that. Just ask Colter, if you need help!"

In a couple of minutes, Smitty was out of sight and Travis's attention turned to the wind. He felt the coolness run into the bones of his small frame, and felt sorry for Smitty having to ride in such weather. He also thought Smitty must be the closest thing to a real mountain man he had ever seen. He liked Smitty and he didn't even mind being teased a bit about Colter.

"Only about an hour of daylight left," his father said. "You want to check the timber above camp here for elk?"

Travis thought it would surely be a waste of time, but nodded his head yes, anyway.

He was right. The timber yielded no elk and, by the time they got back to camp, it was an hour after dark. The wind showed no sign of letting up as it often does around sundown. It seemed to be blowing even harder now, Travis thought as he heated up some stew for dinner.

"We are gonna hunt in the morning, aren't we, Dad?" he asked.

"We shouldn't, but we will. Just for a couple of hours, though," his father replied.

"Well, let's get to sleep early then, so we won't be tired in the morning!"

CHAPTER 19

Even though he was very tired, Travis barely slept this night. He was overwhelmed by disappointment and lay awake most of the night wondering what the morning would bring. More disappointment? Would they have to go home without the huge bull elk he had guaranteed everyone that they would get? Maybe, just maybe, first thing in the morning they would get lucky and find one of the huge bulls they had seen, he thought. But, just as quickly, he wondered if he would have to go home embarrassed to face all he had bragged to. For the first time since he mentioned the trip, he wished that he had heeded his father's words of advice and hadn't boasted and bragged so much.

Travis was awake enough of the night that he was able to keep the stove fired up and the tent didn't get cold. His sleeping bag was warm, and he wondered if maybe Smitty had been wrong. Maybe the weather was not going to turn bad at all. Maybe they should stay, he thought. But he knew his father would never stay after talking to Smitty, so Travis buried the thought of staying deep in the back of his mind. He lay in his bag for the whole night feeling tired, but he could not make his mind quit thinking long enough for his body to relax and sleep.

His mind worked on and on. Several times Travis thought he had fallen asleep, but he didn't know for sure because his mind would just not shut off. The sound of the wind roaring over the trees above camp and the waving canvas of the tent did not help with the sleep issue, either.

The night was long, but finally his father rolled over and said, "Time to wake up." Travis didn't have to wake up. He only had to get up. It took them no time at all to get ready to go ride this morning. The routine of grabbing some food to munch on and getting Skeeter and Annie ready to go had become familiar to both of them. Now Travis was actually a lot of help. He had learned a lot in the past few days, but he was still very worried that it was going to end without an elk.

It was the continuous thinking about going home without a bull that fueled the rage that was building inside him. He wondered and began to doubt whether his father cared about getting an elk at all. "Perhaps he's trying to teach me a lesson about bragging," Travis thought. It seemed awfully cruel and senseless to Travis. As they rode along in the darkness, he became very mad—mad at his father. Angry because Dad hadn't shot one of the two bulls they had seen that very first morning. Travis kept working the events of the hunt through his mind and was fully convinced that his dad would be the only reason that this trip failed.

He had become so consumed by his thoughts toward his father that he didn't even notice that the wind had quit blowing and it was calm out for the first time in two days. He only heard a couple of words when his father said, "Must be the calm before the storm, huh?"

Travis didn't reply. He only scowled. But it was too dark for anyone to see his angry face and, for the first time since this trip began, he secretly wished his father could see how mad he was. "Maybe he would get a clue if he knew!" he thought.

"I figure if we get to that U-shaped meadow before daylight, we've got a chance. If we don't see anything in the meadow, we'll work some of the game trails in the timber," Dad said. Travis still didn't reply.

"You sleepin' back there?"

"No!" Travis retorted in the sharpest tone he could muster. He wanted Dad to know that he was unhappy about all of this.

"A little growly this mornin', are we?" his father responded with a sarcastic chuckle.

"Yeah!" Travis replied. "I don't know why we're even bothering this morning. We aren't gonna see or shoot any elk anyway. We oughta just go home!" he blurted, nearly in tears.

His father stopped Skeeter, and Annie stopped right behind him. Travis became very alert as he watched the outline of Skeeter turn and face him. Then it came.

"You know, maybe—not maybe—definitely, we should be heading down out of these mountains right now. We shouldn't be out here doin' what we are. You ain't never seen the snow up here when it gets after it for a few days!" Matt didn't let up for a second. He continued lecturing in that temperamental voice of his, which he only used when someone really ticked him off.

"Here I am, draggin' my ungrateful snot-nosed kid out one more time and you don't appreciate it! The only thing you're here for on this whole trip is to kill. It's not killin', it's *hunting*! If it were just killing, I, for one, wouldn't be here." By now he was nearly hollering.

"Do you wanta go on, or turn around and head home? It's up to you."

Travis was humbled by the lecture and said in a quiet tone, "Go on."

The horses turned and neither rider said another word until they were near the U-shaped meadow. Travis thought about how he was probably wrong. Well, maybe just a little wrong. After all, what could his father do about the change in the weather? "Nothing at all," he admitted to himself.

Matt was also thinking that maybe he had been wrong. After all, he had known Travis's only objective for this hunt, and he could have fulfilled his son's dream. "Maybe I should have," he thought.

As they neared the meadow it was still dark. Matt turned to Travis and whispered, "Let's wait here for daylight. Maybe they'll bugle."

Travis replied, "Okay." He was still sort of mad, but not like he had been earlier.

"We'll get one this mornin'."

"Think so?"

"Yeah. Yeah, we'll do it today."

Travis had a glimmer of hope. He knew that when his dad said something, he meant it. And he was sure glad his father had finally come to his senses!

With the loss of the wind, Travis knew that the elk would be active this morning, working the meadows, grazing. Perhaps the two bulls would even show again!

They sat for about fifteen minutes hearing nothing. No elk this morning. At least, none that were near enough to hear.

It was exceptionally cool this morning and, as the sun began to peek up in the eastern sky, Travis could see thick, heavy frost on the grass and brush in the meadow. The sight of the frost made him feel even colder. His teeth began to chatter. What little breeze there was easily worked through his heavy clothing and chilled him to the bone. He wanted to get up and move, but he didn't. He just sat and suffered through the silent, frozen morning.

Finally Matt stood up and gestured for Travis to do the same. Travis wasted no time getting up off the cold ground. The two moved along the edge of the timber quietly, watching and listening. As they proceeded, Travis wondered if Dad had heard his teeth chattering and, if so, was that the reason they were now on the move? Or, did his father have a plan? He couldn't ask now because he knew that a person did not talk while hunting or stalking. Besides that, he wasn't even sure that they were on good speaking terms just yet.

They pressed on, working the edge of the meadow, always staying just far enough inside the timber that they could not be easily seen. They had worked their way around to the end of the meadow where the elk had exited that first morning, and still no sight of the elk.

The sky had a hazy overcast to it this morning and, when Travis saw his father looking up at it, he knew that this hunt could be over any minute. Travis's anger toward his dad began to build again. When the older man looked down at his son, he could see it in the boy's facial expression. He didn't say anything. He just quietly pressed on.

At the north end of the meadow, they came to a heavily traveled game trail. It worked its way up into the heavy timber on a hogback between two fingers of black timber. They stopped and Matt said quietly, "We'll work our way up through the timber. Stay close. Oh, and keep your eyes open."

Travis nodded and they started up the trail. The dirt on the trail was ground up quite well. It was also a bit moist, making it very easy to walk and stalk noiselessly. They moved slowly up the hill, watching and listening for elk.

They were just about to the top of a steep pull in the trail when the timber above them came to life. They could hear elk scattering only forty or fifty yards ahead, their feet thumping on the ground and clicking and banging off trees and logs. "They're sure noisy animals!" Travis thought. "They should be easy to find."

At the sound of the elk, the two stopped and listened for just a second, and then ran to the top of the ridge where the noise was coming from. They were too late. The elk had seen them before they saw the elk, and had vanished into the safety of the timber below them. Travis recognized the smell of the elk. It was the same as it had been when they had run into that small group the day they had packed in. "The elk must have lain and bedded on this rise for hours," he thought. He would never forget this smell!

Travis and his dad were both huffing and puffing and gasping for air when they finally stopped. The combination of the high altitude and the steep climb had really heated them up. Travis was actually sweating!

After they had regained their breath, Matt pointed to an outcropping of rocks about a half mile above them and said, "If we move quickly and circle around above the elk, we might get up there in time to see them if they cross."

Now they ran again. Not a fast run, but more of a quick trot. After only a couple of minutes they slowed down, once again gasping for air. They walked for a few minutes. Travis could feel the sweat running down his back. He was thinking, "Let's hurry!" when, suddenly, his dad picked up the pace again. They began to run a bit faster as the trail became less steep.

The excitement was growing in Travis's mind as he ran. He hoped they would beat the elk to the crossing! He was wondering if one of the big bulls would be with this group when, suddenly, his father stopped dead in his tracks causing Travis to run into him and fall to the ground.

He was trying to get up when he saw the fear in his father's eyes. Travis knew something was wrong, *very* wrong!

CHAPTER 20

Immediately, Travis looked up the trail. About ten yards in front of them lay the mutilated body of a dead bull elk. He wondered if it could be the bull that had been gored in the meadow. The smell was terrible. It was the unmistakable stench of a half-rotted dead animal.

When Travis glanced up, he saw that look in his father's eyes again. Matt hadn't said a word. He only motioned for Travis to back down the trail, as he jacked a shell into the chamber of the 300 magnum. As Travis watched the shell slide into the chamber, he suddenly realized the danger they were facing. They had come across a bear kill, and the bear was probably nearby! Travis knew that this time of year the bears go into a feeding frenzy and do not take kindly to others invading their space, especially when it involves their food.

Travis began to back up as fast as he could. He was afraid, and wanted to get out of this jam as quickly as possible.

Suddenly, out of the dark timber along the trail, the bear appeared! It had been only ten or fifteen yards from where they had stopped. The bear didn't stand up or roar at them. It simply advanced to the trail. Perhaps it hadn't seen them, Travis thought. But this thought had barely cleared his mind when the bear charged. Matt yelled, "Run, Travis!" Then he began screaming and hollering at the bear.

Travis ran about ten steps and turned to see his father raise the rifle and shoot. The shot was loud, and was followed immediately by another. Then there was a short pause and a third shot. The bear was not even slowed by the onslaught of rifle fire.

Thousands of thoughts rushed through Travis's mind in just seconds. "What should I do?" he wondered. "Should I run? What can I do?" Fear had paralyzed him and he could do nothing. He only watched helplessly as the bear hit his father with fierce wild fury. It flung him through the air like a grown man tossing a bag of flour. The bear pounced on him again, clawing and biting with tremendous power.

Matt screamed again. This time it was a scream of terror and pain.

Travis was hiding behind a tree in his own terror, listening. He peeked out from behind it as he watched the brutal mauling. His father's body had gone limp now, and Travis started to back down the hill. The bear was still in his vision and Travis was about to turn and run when, as quickly as it had begun, the mauling ended. The huge bear released his father and darted off into the heavy timber.

Travis froze in his tracks. He stood motionless for several minutes wondering if he should approach his father, or if he should run for help. His father's body showed no sign of life. Travis was afraid to approach the body. "What if the bear is just over the edge waiting for its next victim?" he thought. "Or, worse yet, what if Dad is dead?" Tears streamed down his face, but he made no sound as he wondered what to do.

Travis wanted to run for help, but who would he find? He hadn't seen another person, other than Smitty, since he had been here, and he didn't know where Smitty would be now.

The man whom Travis had always thought of as being indestructible still lay motionless only thirty yards in front of him, and Travis couldn't work up the nerve to walk up and see if he were dead or alive. He was positive that his father was dead. At least, that was how it appeared. He couldn't clear his mind to make the right decision. "Run, or stay?" ran through his mind time after time. He couldn't calm himself down enough to even think rationally. Fear had possessed him. He tried to calm his mind, but the attempts were futile. Screaming and crying would be much easier now, but he was at least rational enough to keep the silence.

Standing there unable to make a decision, not knowing what to do, seemed eternal. "What could I possibly do?" he thought. "Could I even help?" But then something his father had once said to him flashed through his mind. "Never leave a partner in a bind."

"This is the only way," Travis thought, and he began to approach the motionless body. He moved cautiously and slowly closer, attempting to gather his thoughts and prepare for the worst.

"Okay," he thought. "First thing I need to do is get the rifle and reload it, just in case." He was only fifteen yards away now, and he burst forward at a sprint trying to spot the rifle as he ran. It was lying on the ground about fifteen yards up the trail, so Travis sprinted on past his father, not even looking down at him as he went by. He didn't want to look. For this moment, he only wanted the safety of the rifle.

When he reached the rifle, he quickly snatched it up and pulled the bolt back to eject the spent cartridge. He locked a new one into the chamber as he moved back toward his father, surveying the surrounding timber for any movement.

When he was over his father's body, he still couldn't look. Instead, he reached for his father's ammo belt, grabbing it and pulling cartridges out of it, working with his hands and constantly looking for the bear. When he had about a half dozen shells out of the belt, he fumbled with the clip in the rifle. When he finally had it removed, he started inserting shells. It held four rounds. When he finally had them in the clip, he slammed it back into the rifle.

Now he had to look. He didn't want to, but he slowly raised his head, telling himself that he must be strong and he must keep his wits about him. His father's jacket sleeves were shredded, but there only appeared to be slight puncture wounds under them. Then his eyes continued upward, looking at the neck and face.

Blood was everywhere, and the sight of it made Travis nauseous. He turned away nearly starting to vomit, trying not to, and telling himself, "I gotta be strong! Gotta be tough! Strong! Tough!" over and over. Finally, his eyes wincing, he turned, determined to face the problem and make the right decision.

Fear of the bear had left him for the moment. Now he only feared for his father's life. If Dad was alive, he would stay with him and do all he could to help him.

His father's face was a ghastly sight, showing several deep claw wounds and multiple tooth punctures. Travis stiffened, gathered his feelings, and began to think. He realized that it was mostly blood that made his father's face look so bad. Perhaps the wounds were not as severe as they could have been. Travis reached down and put his hand on his father's throat, checking for a pulse. He thought he could feel one, but he wasn't sure if it was his own heart pounding that he felt, or his father's. Now he was sure. It was his father's!

Relief filled Travis's entire body. He began by taking his bandana off and soaking it with water from his canteen to wipe some of the blood from his father's face. He worked quickly, diligently, and thoughtfully, wondering what he should do next.

Suddenly, the injured man's arms twitched. He moaned, and Travis could see his eyes moving underneath his closed eyelids. Travis prodded him now, and though it took several minutes, his father's eyes finally opened and stared up at him. He said nothing. He just stared at Travis for a long time.

Travis figured the bear had knocked him unconscious and that his father would get his bearings any moment now and they could be on their way.

"You okay?" Travis asked repeatedly. "You okay?"

Finally his father moaned, "Maybe," as he reached up to touch Travis. "Terrible pain in my back."

The tears flowed again as Travis bent over to hug his father. He could feel that this man was in severe pain. "Can you walk?"

"I don't know. Don't think so," was his father's reply.

"Move your legs," Travis yelled as he watched for movement. But there was none.

All he heard was, "I can't."

Anxiety began to build in Travis once again. "How am I going to get you out of here?"

"I don't know. We'll work something out, though," Matt replied in a gasping voice. He was trying to hide the pain and severity of the situation from his son, but not successfully. Travis could see that they had a very serious problem at hand, and worked to collect his thoughts as he spoke. "Must have hurt your back when that bear flung ya, huh?"

"Yeah. Where is the bear?" his father asked with intense concern.

"Down there, somewhere," Travis answered as he pointed down to the dark timber below them.

"Probably dead, huh?"

"Yeah," Travis replied. "Probably dead."

"What time is it?"

"I don't know for sure. Maybe nine or nine-thirty."

"Travis, listen to me," his father said, wincing with pain. "You have to go get help. Run back to the horses and ride as fast as you can to get help. Not so fast that you end up hurt, but hurry!"

"I will. I'll hurry," Travis said as he put the rifle in his father's arms.

"Be tough, Boy, just like Colter!" his father said, trying to force a smile.

"I'll be back!" Travis called as he turned to run down the mountain to where the horses were tied. He thought that it was a terrible time for his father to pop a joke, but he knew why he had done it. It was called psychology, and though Travis didn't know much about it, he did know that grown-ups used it a lot.

Travis ran as hard as he could, partly to put distance between himself and the bear, and partly because he knew it would be necessary to get help as quickly as possible.

He had started to slow down a bit from fatigue when his mind turned to Colter. He remembered that the mountain man had once outrun an entire tribe of Blackfoot Indians. Now Travis hoped that he could outrun the clock. The clock, in his case, was the amount of time he figured his father could survive up there all by himself with only his arms and knowledge to help him. Travis quickened his pace and, though he was gasping for air, he kept running. Now he knew how Colter had felt, and he was just as determined to win this race against the clock as Colter had been to win his race against the Indians.

CHAPTER 21

The run back to the horses proved to be the perfect medicine for clearing Travis's mind and getting him back on the road to thinking in a manner which would be productive for saving time as well as his father's life. As he cleared the woods entering the meadow, he stopped, realizing that this would be a hard spot to find again. Reaching into his day pack, he pulled out a roll of fluorescent marking ribbon. He tore off two long pieces and tied them to the limbs of a blue spruce tree to mark the spot where the trail left the meadow.

Once again he was on the run across the meadow, now in the open. As he ran, he was thinking about his next decision. Leaving one of the horses tied where they were would help him find that spot more quickly. But, which one would he leave? Skeeter was faster, having the thoroughbred blood in him, but Annie was geared up for him and probably had more stamina for the long ride out.

The decision was made by the time he reached the horses. Quickly he tied another piece of the ribbon on the tree next to Skeeter, just in case the horse might break loose and run off. Then he tightened the cinch down on Annie and rode off.

By now he was very familiar with the trail and made good time heading back to camp. Trying to come up with a plan to find help led him to a discovery that nearly put him in shock again. The sky seemed even darker now than it had been, and the air was beginning to cool down again, too.

What concerned Travis most, though, was where he was going to find help. Smitty had said that he was headed toward the thoroughfare, and Travis had no idea how to even begin looking for him.

The snow was not supposed to hit them for a day or two, but it looked to Travis as though it could start snowing at any time. He thought if he headed back down the main trail toward the trailhead, he might find another camp, or other hunters Smitty had talked to, heading out. But what if he didn't? What if he had to ride all the way to the trailhead for help? At the pace he was traveling now, he would be riding until well after dark. At best it would be morning, probably late morning, before anyone could get back, and that would be only if the weather cooperated and they were able to fly in with a helicopter.

"What if the weather turns bad? What if I can't get back?" He was still asking himself questions as Annie came to their camp. He jumped off the horse to get a bit of food and water for the ride toward the trailhead.

He was gathering some goodies to shove into his pack when he suddenly stopped. It shocked him and made his whole body quiver and break out in goose bumps when the realization struck him. His father had sent him out to find help, not to save himself, but more to save Travis! Travis was certain that this was his father's plan. It made him almost mad to think that his own father would do such a thing to him. It was going to be cold this night. Dad would probably not even survive the night in his weakened condition. Travis was sure of it! The anxiety built inside him, growing until he could control it no more. He screamed "Aughhhh . . . !" over and over, loud, louder than the howling coyotes in the early evening. He screamed at the sky. And when it was all over, he prayed for help.

He wasn't leaving. He was going to help his father. He wasn't sure what he would do, but he wasn't leaving! He knew this for sure. "Never leave a friend or a partner in a bind," he recalled. It was his father's own saying.

How would he do it, though, he wondered. Travis wished Jess were here. His brother would know what to do.

Travis was outside the tent scrounging through camping equipment, throwing into a pile anything he thought might be useful: extra rope, a hatchet, lighting fluid, a saw, and whatever else he could find. He still had no plan.

He stood nearly in panic wondering what to do when he saw someone squatting in the lodge pole shelter. He ran toward it yelling, "I
need help! My dad's been attacked by a bear. Help me!" But as he
approached the shelter, he realized that no one was there. "Imagination. My imagination!" He thought, "Maybe it was Colter. No! No!"
He had been teased so much about Colter that he wanted to just forget
about him, but he couldn't.

"What would Colter do?" he wondered. Then the idea hit him! He
would take the ladder they had built and make a travois like the Indians used to use for packing things. "It'll work," he thought. "Buck will
pull it back down here." He hollered, "Thanks, Colter!" as he began to
load everything he would need onto Buck.

In no time at all he had Buck loaded and was ready to head back
up the trail. But first, he had to leave a note. A note to let anyone
happening by, maybe even Smitty, know that there was trouble and he
needed help. The note read:

> To Smitty or anyone else: I think my dad broke his back
> when a bear attacked him. I'm going to get him out. Please
> come and help me. Go about two miles north on the main
> trail, then left up the hill. I'll mark the way with orange rib-
> bon.
> Please hurry!
> Travis Driskoll

Travis didn't know if anyone could follow his directions or, for that
matter, if anyone would even stop to see them, but he would mark a
good trail just in case. He was glad, now, that Dad had brought the
journal and pencils.

After the note was stuck to the tent with some tape from his pack,
he jumped back on Annie and grabbed Buck's lead rope. Travis could
see that Annie was tired, but he pushed her on at a trot. They couldn't
travel much faster because of the awkward load on Buck. To move any
faster would cause the load to tip, and valuable time would be lost
trying to reload him.

Travis had forgotten to check the time, and he wondered how late
it was as he marked the spot where they left the main trail and headed

up. He also worried about how his father was doing. He hoped the injured man would be strong enough to help. Maybe he would be able to pull himself onto the travois when Travis had it built. He also hoped that the snow wouldn't come today, but it looked like it might.

Finally Travis saw Skeeter and realized that he was going to have to go back up that hill—that hill which may have a wounded grizzly bear hiding on it, laying an ambush for the next intruder.

His fear was great, but his desire to help his father was greater. As he tied Annie beside Skeeter, he grabbed the 25-06 and pulled it out of the scabbard. He couldn't take Annie any farther. He would walk now, leading Buck, with the rifle flung over his shoulder. He didn't know what good the rifle would do if he did have a run-in with the bear, but somehow he felt a bit more secure having it with him.

As he led Buck through the patch of timber between the other horses and the meadow, he marked trees with the orange tape, leaving a trail he thought anyone could follow.

Finally he came to the spot where he had to leave the meadow to head up the trail through the timber to where he had left his father. His heart began to pound harder than ever, and his throat felt dry as he gasped for air. He didn't want to go back up there, but he had no choice. He didn't hesitate or even consider slowing. He just moved on.

His dad was only about a half mile away now, and Travis was sure it was afternoon. He tried to hurry. The trail seemed much more eerie now, and Travis heard every noise in the woods around him. Every time a squirrel chattered or a bird chirped, he would look to see what it was. He was overly jumpy and he knew it. He didn't stop or slow to see what the noises were. If anything, he moved faster—as fast as Buck could move up the hill. Travis's guts were in a knot when a limb popped below him. He almost wanted to turn around and go back, but he didn't. He was getting close, and he pulled on Buck's lead rope as hard as he could.

CHAPTER 22

As Travis approached his father, he could see him struggling to look around, trying to see what was coming up the trail. Travis hollered, "It's just me, Dad!" He could see his father relax and settle down as he recognized the voice.

As they got closer, Buck could smell the dead elk and the bear. He became very reluctant to proceed, pulling back and wanting to stop. Travis figured that he would tie Buck up a distance away from the scent and give him time to get used to it. Buck was a mild mannered horse, and Travis figured he would be okay in a few minutes, once he became accustomed to the smell.

Immediately, Travis pulled the ladder and the rest of the load off Buck and started dragging it up toward his father. As he got close, he asked, "Are ya okay?"

The reply was, "Yeah," but they both knew better.

Dad's face had swelled while he was gone, but the sight of it didn't seem to affect Travis as much as it had at first.

"Did you bring help?" his father asked in a low, painful voice.

"No," Travis replied. "Where would I find it?"

"I told you . . ."

Travis cut him off and let loose with some of the pent up feelings he had tried to bury deep inside himself. "Yeah. You told me!" Tears were building in his glassed over eyes. "You told me to leave. Leave you in a bind! You said, 'Run away. Go get yourself safe. I'll lay here and die while you think you're off trying to get help.' I'm not dumb!" he added.

"Okay," his father said, but Travis wouldn't stop.

"Look at you! You'd a died tonight out here in the cold. It's gonna snow. I saw you wantin' to say it this mornin', you know."

This time Matt cut him off. "Well, ya got a plan?"

"Yeah."

"Well?"

"I brought the ladder and Buck. Gonna make a travois with the poles and a sleeping bag. All you gotta do is help pull yourself up on it when it's ready. Okay?"

"Okay," was the reply. Travis went to work immediately, disassembling the ladder. He kept looking down the hill every once in a while to make sure Buck was all right. He talked to his father as he worked. When the ladder poles were free, he grabbed the heavy flannel sleeping bag and stuck the poles inside of it. Now he took his knife and cut two holes for the poles to go through. It seemed as though he were taking forever to get done, but Travis wanted the travois to be sturdy enough that it wouldn't fall apart once his father was loaded onto it.

Next he needed two new rungs, because the old ones he had cut off were not wide enough. A green sapling near the trail would be long enough for both the top and bottom rungs. Travis sawed furiously. He wanted to get done and out of here! Though he was progressing at a quick pace, it did not seem fast enough to him. He pulled the saw back and forth until he was nearly all the way through, then finished it off by bending it over toward the ground with all his might. The small camping axe quickly cleaned off all the limbs, and Travis was ready to measure and notch. The notching went quickly and, in no time, Travis had tied the bottom rung on. He sawed it to the right length and went to work on the top rung, talking as he worked.

"How we gonna get you on here and get this thing hooked up to Buck?" he asked as he worked. When there was no response, Travis glanced over to see his father's eyes closed. But Travis knew he wasn't sleeping. He was thinking.

Travis worked for several more minutes. Then he heard, "How much rope ya bring?"

"A lot," Travis responded.

"You about done?"

"Yeah, about."

Travis kept at it, working frantically cutting holes through the bag and tying it to the side poles and the top and bottom rungs. He thought it had to be getting toward mid afternoon, and it was getting colder. He could see his breath for the first time since morning. There was no time to waste, he thought as he finished up his masterpiece. "Done!" he hollered as he finished.

His father nodded his head in approval as Travis looked at him and waited for instruction. "Get the heavy rope," was the first order.

Travis got the rope and was once again standing over his wounded father.

"Listen now," Matt said. "Throw the rope up over the limb above me and bring your carrier over here."

Travis knew what to do now. He grabbed the travois and laid it down parallel to his father. Then he threw the rope over about a four inch limb that hung directly above his father and about three branches up from the bottom. The limb would be strong enough to support the weight of the travois until he had it hooked to the pack saddle. When he had both sides attached to a rope, he looked at his father and asked, "Ya ready?"

His father nodded, and Travis grabbed hold of his legs. Then he let go and said, "Wait."

"What?" his father moaned.

"What if I hurt you worse when I move you?" Travis asked.

"Don't worry. I don't think it can hurt much worse. Let me pull the front part of my body over first, then you do the legs."

With a mighty grunt, his father did just that, moving his body over and wincing in pain. Travis immediately pushed the lower half of his body over. It was done! But the sight of causing someone such pain almost made his nauseous again. Travis began to fall apart, laying his head on his father's chest and crying, "I'm sorry. I'm sorry. I'm sorry!"

Then he felt two hands come up and wrap themselves around his back. A voice whispered, "You're the best darn twelve-year-old I've ever known. Now, stop cryin' and get Buck up here. You're doin' good. Be tough, like Colter!"

"Okay," he sobbed and gave his father a gentle hug. Then he went to retrieve Buck. The horse had adjusted to the smell fairly well, and offered very little resistance to advancing up the trail.

This is what had always made Buck such a wonderful pack horse. He adapted to every situation and was always reliable. Travis led him right up to the travois and tied him to a sapling. Then he watched cautiously for a few seconds until the horse sent his nose to the ground and began to eat.

Travis asked, "What now?"

"You pick up on the poles and I'll pull on the ropes until we can tie this thing off," his father replied.

Travis thought that they weren't very clear directions, but he knew what he had to do. He grabbed hold of the fronts of the poles and lifted with all his might. He grunted and lifted as his father pulled on the ropes with his arms. They struggled to get it shoulder high on Travis and then Travis heard, "Can ya hold while I tie it?"

"Yes," he groaned. And he did it! It was perhaps the most strenuous task Travis had ever performed, but he did it.

After lifting the travois, hooking it up to the pack saddle was a piece of cake. Now he only needed to pack the rifles and they were ready to travel.

With one rifle strapped to the pack saddle and the other one on his shoulder, Travis took the lead rope and started down the trail with Buck and the travois following. He thought to himself that he had done a good job. But more importantly, he had done the right thing.

They had gone about thirty yards when Travis stopped Buck and walked back to see how his creation was holding together. "How ya doin' back here?" he asked as he approached the travois.

"I've done better," was the reply. "But it's pretty good ridin'."

"Holler if it gets too rough."

His father nodded okay, and Travis walked up front again, leading the horse down the trail at a slow walk.

Travis made it down to the meadow without incident. The trail was steep, but it was also wide and free of downfall timber. He had also made it without running into the bear that had attacked his father, or any other bear, the thing he now feared most.

But his second worst fear was now turning into reality—snow! Just a few flakes every now and then, but Travis knew by looking at the sky that more would follow. He had to make better time. Yet, it seemed impossible without hurting his father. He walked across the meadow as fast as he could without bouncing the travois. Travis knew it had to be painful for his father, but the man never complained. At the same time, he knew he had to get up the steep trail beyond Annie and Skeeter before it got too wet and muddy—or too dark!

The timber between the meadow and the other two horses posed challenge after challenge. It was not a great distance—perhaps only a hundred yards—but there was no trail, and downed timber covered the forest floor. Each time they came to a fallen tree, Travis would stop Buck and inch him forward in an attempt to ease the travois over the logs. It worked each time, but it also took precious time—perhaps a half hour—to move a mere one hundred yards.

Finally, Travis caught sight of Annie and Skeeter and headed straight for them. The flurries were coming more often now, and it was only a matter of time before the all-out snow would set in and start to accumulate on the ground. Travis stopped Buck and ran over to Skeeter. He untied the horse, pulled his bridle off, and tied it to his saddle horn. Then he grabbed a bedroll that was tied to the back of the saddle. He ran and covered his father with the wool blanket and asked, "You okay?"

His father nodded "yes." Travis ran up to Annie, checked the cinch, jumped on her back, grabbed Buck's lead rope and they were off!

As they moved toward the steep part of the trail, the snow began to come down harder. It was also getting heavier and wetter and starting to stick to the brush and stems of grass along the trail. Darkness was setting in, yet Travis could see that the ground below him was getting slick. He was helpless to change the situation, though. This was the only way back, and the horses could only ascend at the speed they were now moving. To travel any faster would surely cause a wreck, hurting one of the horses, or Travis, or his father—again.

The pull was difficult but the caravan continued. Skeeter followed, and Travis hoped he didn't follow too closely. "What if Buck stumbled or stopped? Skeeter might walk right up on the travois! No, relax," he told himself. "Skeeter can see a lot better than me." He knew that

Skeeter would not step on his father, yet that thought preoccupied his mind.

Now they were on the rise just below the steepest part of the climb. "Only sixty yards to go," Travis thought. But how could he make it? It was totally black out now, and the snow was coming heavier. "What if the horses wander off the trail?" Travis didn't know what to do! The only thing he knew was that doing nothing would be the wrong thing.

He thought for a few seconds. Then he remembered his brother, Jess, telling him about a time when he had been out sheep hunting and had to ride through a white out to get back to camp. Jess and his partner had to get off their horses and had no idea where they were. They made their way back to camp by holding on to their horses' tails and letting the horses find the way. Jess had said, "They knew where the groceries were!"

Travis jumped off Annie and worked his way back to Skeeter. Skeeter had been up this trail many times, and he surely knew the way. He didn't say a word as the walked past the travois. "No sense in worryin' him anymore today," Travis thought.

He got Skeeter to the front and Annie to the rear, grabbed Skeeter by the tail and mushed him on. Skeeter was eager to lead and practically dragged Travis up the hill at a bit faster pace than Travis really wanted to go. Buck followed. Travis was sure the ride was too rough for his father, but he had no control over the pace. It was determined by the amount of struggling each horse had to do in order to lunge forward and climb up at the same time.

Travis had been nervous about going down this part of the trail that first morning when he could at least see a little bit. Now his eyes were useless. The combination of cloud cover and heavy snow made it impossible for him to even see his own hands. It was completely dark. Travis could just as well be a blind man. For sure, he did not want to lose Buck's lead rope. The horse could be five feet away and Travis would never find him if he lost that rope! And there was no way he would let go of Skeeter. As a matter of fact, he wished he had put a lead rope on Skeeter also, just as an added safety device.

Skeeter was the guide on this evening. Skeeter pulled and Travis held on. It was a job just keeping his feet under himself, slipping in the greasy mud on the trail, or tripping over a rock or piece of brush off to the side of the trail. Travis had no idea if they had gone twenty of the sixty yards, or fifty-nine of them, but he prayed for safety at the top.

When they finally did top out, he thought it felt more like a mile than sixty yards! It was such a huge relief to safely make it to the top of this hill that Travis felt almost totally secure. He forgot for a moment that he, a mere twelve-year-old, was all alone. That is, all alone with a crippled father who may have life threatening injuries, probably at the least, a broken back. Travis was alone, and at the mercy of a horse to help him find his way back to camp on a night when the human eye was useless, in one of the most remote areas in the lower forty-eight states.

If he had thought about all of that, he probably would have fallen apart again. But he didn't. He rested with the horses and celebrated the safe climb to the top on this darkest of nights, in the worst of conditions. He figured the next couple of miles would be easy if he delegated the authority to Skeeter.

Travis was not afraid of the dark tonight. Not because he had overcome the fear by some fabulous remedy, but rather, because he had forgotten about it. Too many other things roamed into his mind.

CHAPTER 23

Skeeter and Buck proved to be the champions of the evening. Skeeter took the group straight back to camp in the blinding snow, never letting on that he was the least bit unsure about how to get there. Buck followed, pulling the cumbersome load at a steady pace, never halting, always keeping up.

Travis thought the snow was turning into all that Smitty had said it would be. In the time it had taken the group to travel the two miles, Travis estimated that four to six inches had piled up on the ground.

When Skeeter stopped, Travis reached into his fanny pack and pulled out some matches. Lighting one after another, he finally located the tent and headed Skeeter and Buck toward it.

Now he needed another plan. How was he going to get his father inside the tent? Travis thought about this new dilemma as he untied the tent flap and entered. The first thing he did was to light the lantern. He desperately needed to get his father inside and get the fire going so they could warm up. The wet snow had melted on his shoulders and back, and he was beginning to feel very chilled.

There wasn't room enough to lead Buck in, unhook him from the travois, and lead him back out. Travis thought, though, that he might be able to simply back the contraption into the tent. He led Buck up to the open flap, turned him away from it, and lined the travois up with the opening. Then he reached up and pushed on Buck's head and halter, trying to move the horse backward.

Buck backed up, but the poles of the travois only dug into the ground. Then Travis heard a raspy, worn voice saying, "Put some skil . . . under the po . . . ."

Travis didn't understand. Matter of fact, he hadn't heard half of the order. He pulled the wool blanket off his father's face to hear him say again, "Take and put a skillet under each pole."

It registered now, and Travis ran into the tent, got two frying pans and put one under each pole. The pans slid over the ground as Buck backed up, shoving the travois into the tent.

Once it was in position, Travis stopped Buck and wondered what he should do next. "How can I get Buck unhooked and lower the travois?" he wondered. His eyes scanned back and forth across the tent, but could not find what he was looking for. Then he remembered the stacked firewood. He ran and dug through the pile of split wood, looking for pieces that were uniform in size. None of them seemed quite perfect, and he quickly realized that being overly picky at this time was not an option. Hauling pieces of wood inside to build a crib only took a few minutes.

Buck was patient. He barely moved a muscle while Travis worked at assembling the cribs for the poles of the travois to sit on. "The patience of Job," Travis thought as he worked. "Old Buck has the patience of Job . . ." The saying was one he had heard his mother use a thousand times. One of her favorites, Travis thought with a sort of comforting smile on his face. Usually when she used the saying, it was in reference to the patience which was required by herself or others when dealing with Travis!

Suddenly the good thoughts were gone, and Travis remembered that no one, not even his mother or his brother, Jess, knew that there was anything wrong. How could they? Worse yet, he thought, there was no way to let anyone know. This worried him, but right now he had to finish his work and get the tent closed up and a fire going.

Once the cribs were square, level, and positioned, Travis crawled up on Buck's back and prepared to lower his creation. He worried about dropping it too hard and causing pain or greater injury to his father, but this was the only way it could be done. He had to get the tent closed up and warmed up soon, or they would both freeze.

After pulling the rope ends through the slip knots, Travis prepared to pull with all his might. He lowered one side of the travois about six inches. It was not as heavy as he had thought it would be, and the other side went down just as easily.

Travis wasted no time getting Buck out of the tent and getting a fire started in the stove. The first warmth and glow of the crackling pine bark was inviting, and Travis knew his father was in an excellent position to warm up quickly as the stove heated up. He hadn't planned it this way and, if there were such a thing as luck on this terrible day, he was happy that it had happened.

Travis sucked up the warmth from the fire as he gathered his wits and planned his next move. "Let's see," he thought, "gotta take care of the horses yet, and see if Dad's okay or needs anything. Maybe wash him up."

He hadn't looked at his father's face except for a glance when they had talked every once in a while. He didn't want to be sick as he had almost been when he had looked at his father for the first time after the attack. But now he told himself, "Suck it up. Ya gotta do it. Be tough!" He tried to psych himself up for the job which had to be done, but he felt butterflies in his stomach and apprehension in his thoughts.

As he dug for the first aid kit, he told himself over and over, "Just do it! Just do it!" With the kit in his hand, he grabbed one of the plastic water jugs and put a full kettle on to boil. He dug a flannel shirt out to use as a rag.

As he prepared, he thought that maybe he shouldn't do it. Maybe he would just cause his father more pain. Maybe it was too late. But Travis knew the best thing to do was what he was preparing to do.

As he waited for the water to heat, he took off his wet jacket and shirt and put on dry ones. The dry clothes instantly took some of the chill off Travis's body and he knew that, for now, he was safe.

Then the dreaded moment arrived. The water was warm and the job had to be done. Travis slowly reached up and gently pulled the wool blanket off his father, at first not looking at his face, but then finally pulling his eyes off the blanket and looking up. The sight was ghastly. Dad's face was almost solid red with dried and clotted blood.

Travis turned away again, gagging and feeling nauseous. He commanded himself, "Get it over with." Then he took several deep breaths, turned around with the warm, wet rag, and went to work. With the touch of the warm cloth on his face, the man's eyes opened and he began to say something. But Travis calmed him by simply shaking his head and saying, "Shhh."

Travis couldn't talk or listen as he scrubbed. He could barely breathe as the tears began to run down his cheeks. Matt didn't try to speak again as Travis continued his work. He washed gently, yet thoroughly, and each time his father's eyes opened, he would soothe and calm him by saying, "Shhh," or, "Just relax." Travis didn't really know why he did this, but it made him feel more comfortable. He thought about his mother, who had often said the same things to him when he was in need of comfort or love. But she had always added a hug. He couldn't do that right now, at least not while he was working on his father's wounds.

"Use the antiseptic," Travis heard, and he reached into the kit to retrieve it. He rubbed it over the cuts and his father mumbled, "Scrub them out good. Might hurt, but do it anyhow." These were not the words Travis wanted to hear, but he took the peroxide and washed out the cuts, then rubbed antiseptic cream into them one at a time until all of them were clean. The cuts were long and deep, and should require stitches, Travis thought. But for tonight he would get them clean and wrap them with gauze to keep them moist. Perhaps tomorrow there would be help.

Travis was finishing wrapping the wounds when his father whispered, "Don't forget the horses." Then he dozed off to rest.

Travis didn't want to go back outside. This day had seemed never ending, and he only wanted to collapse and collect his thoughts. But he thought about the horses being out in the cold, wet night and decided that they had done much for him this day. He should surely go take care of them.

He stood up, put another piece of wood on the fire, put his father's canvas duster on, and untied the tent flap to enter the snowy, dark night.

The snow was coming down even more heavily now. Buck had moved only a few feet, so Travis went to work pulling the pack saddle off him. He tossed the saddle on the ground by the tent and realized that he could not even see Annie or Skeeter. He couldn't see ten yards, even with the light. Now he was scared. What if he got far enough away from the tent that he couldn't find his way back? Then he remembered what his father had done one time during a blizzard at home when he needed to get to the barn to feed the livestock. Travis grabbed several rolls of nylon rope. He tied one end to a tent stake and began walking in the direction he guessed the horses would be.

He found them standing in under the old lean-to lodge. Colter's lodge, as Travis had come to think of it. He unsaddled the two horses, then wandered around in the dark until he found the other three and led them to the shelter also. He was careful never to let go of his own rope. The tree where the oats were hanging was only a few yards away. Travis didn't waste any time cutting a bag down and feeding his partners in the wilderness. Once done, he reeled himself back into the tent. He was determined that this was where he was going to stay!

Travis loaded the stove again as he entered the tent, then filled the lantern with gas and cleared a spot on the floor to set it. There was no way he was going to shut it off tonight! He justified his decision to leave it burning by thinking, "What if I have to get up to help Dad? Or what if someone rides by? At least, they'd see the tent." The decision was final.

Travis threw some extra jackets and a bag over his resting father. As he headed for his own bag, he looked at the hand-wound alarm clock. It read three-fifteen.

The excitement, terror, fear, and strenuous work of the day had taken its toll. Travis was exhausted. He lay in his bag recounting the terrible events of the day—and fell asleep, almost sobbing.

CHAPTER 24

Sleep was restless and abbreviated. There were many distractions and interruptions on the first night of winter in the high country. First, there were dreams about the bear. Each time, the bear got just a bit closer to Travis before he woke up and realized that it was only a dream. The dreams almost paralyzed Travis as his fear grew to the point he thought his heart would explode. He had never felt so empty and alone and small. Sitting up after the fourth or fifth dream, Travis realized, for the first time in his life, that he was not the center of the universe. He was only a very minute part of it. He felt more like a lonely pebble of sand in a desert than the center of importance he had always considered himself to be.

When the dreams didn't wake him, the conscious need to keep the fire going did. Several times he got up and loaded the small stove, knowing that his father's chances of surviving this ordeal were much better if he were kept warm.

Yet, he wasn't thinking so much about his father. When he was able to release his mind from the dreams, he thought about his mother, Jess, and even Mrs. Goodman. "If only I had stayed in school and not come on this trip!" he thought. "My father would be safe now and . . ." That's when the thought first came to him. He believed it was his fault! "After all, I'm the one who wanted to go out after the elk yesterday morning. I'm the reason my father may be dying or crippled forever!"

Travis sat up in his bag, pulled his knees up to his chin, cupped his hands to his face and sobbed. Not out loud, though. Even in this frame of mind, he would not make noise enough to wake his father. He sobbed on and on, blaming himself for what had happened, wishing he had reacted differently to Smitty's news. It went on for ten, maybe twenty, minutes. Then he began to collect his thoughts again and, though he was not a religious person, he prayed, "God, I've made some mistakes here and done some bad things. But I'm all alone and I need some help. Please, God, send help. And forgive me!"

Travis lay in his bag for a few minutes pondering what his next move would be. He wondered whether or not the bear would be there if he fell asleep. He did not ponder this for long, though. Exhaustion overtook his small body and he was, once again, sleeping.

The bear was not in his dream now, but the dead bull elk was. Travis was standing on top of the elk. He didn't know why. It made no sense. He just stood there staring, with fear in his eyes, at the spot from which the bear had appeared and attacked his father.

As he stared, he wondered if he were actually there in body, or just in spirit. He could not feel his physical being, but he didn't know for sure. Fear had again paralyzed him and, though he desperately wanted to leave, he could not.

Then he heard a sound. At first it was just grass and weeds moving. Once in a while a twig would pop. "Just the noises of squirrels or any number of other things," he told himself. He was still standing either on, or above, the bull. It was all confusing! "Am I on the bull or above him? And why can't I leave?" he asked his subconscious. Still he had no answers, and no ability to leave.

The noises grew closer and closer, consuming every bit of his attention now. His mind struggled and urged him to leave, but his body did not move. A large, black outline began to take shape just inside the already dark timber. "Why can't I run? Why did I come back here? Why didn't I bring a rifle?" He asked the questions over and over as he tossed and turned in his sleep.

The bear stood just inside the timber, not making any aggressive moves toward him, simply showing that it was present. "Toying with me," Travis thought. Each knew the other's location, yet neither took any action to leave or attack. It was the stalemate of stalemates! Travis was beginning to lose this mind game with the bear. He fought to leave, but he didn't move.

Then the bear showed its face, intimidating Travis even more than before. The two ice cold, dark, beady eyes stared at him with a hate Travis had never seen or felt in his life. He knew that he should have left earlier. He wondered why he couldn't. It didn't matter, though, because now Travis was sure that he would be this bear's next meal. As quickly as this thought went through his mind, he screamed at the bear, "Go ahead! C'mon! Eat me!"

With that invitation, the bear's eyes lit up. Its mouth opened, showing off what appeared to be six-inch canines and a bloody, red tongue. Its piercing roar quieted the whole forest as it lunged on the attack. With one slow motion leap after another, it kept moving closer and closer.

Travis still couldn't move. He just stood there waiting for the inevitable. "Perhaps one more leap," he thought as the bear's face grew larger and larger. In the time it had taken the bear to make the four or five leaps from the edge of the timber to the spot where Travis stood, he had seen most of the good things that had happened to him in his lifetime. Not only had he seen them, he had felt them, heard them, even smelled them! Some of the things he had forgotten long ago. In short, his life had passed before his own eyes. He wondered if he were dead! "Perhaps my heart quit before the bear got me," he thought. Looking up into the bear's eyes, though, answered his question. It would be one more lunge.

Just as the bear was about to hit him, Travis heard another noise off to his left. "Aye Ahh!" roared a tall man wearing buckskins. "Uhhng!" He smashed into the side of the bear, rolling it as the two collided. The bear roaring and the man roaring wreaked havoc in Travis's mind. The commotion was incomprehensible! But, when it was all over, the bear ran off. The man stood up, turned to face Travis, and said, "Howdy! John Colter to your rescue!"

CHAPTER 25

After the dream, Travis slept well. Perhaps too well. When his eyes opened, he could tell it was daylight. When he checked the alarm clock, it said 11:40. As he unzipped his bag, he heard a voice. "Didn't think you was gonna get up today."

Travis's first thought was, "Is it Colter?" but at the same instant he realized it was the voice of his father. He quickly responded, "Sorry! Guess I was tired."

"That's okay."

"Should've hollered. I'd have gotten up."

"Been awake since *you* hollered. Have a bad dream?" his dad asked, wincing a bit from the pain.

Travis thought, "No need in worrying him anymore," and started to say no. But he thought better of it and admitted, "Yeah. Well, kinda."

"What do ya mean, 'kinda'?"

Travis stuck his head out of the tent to check the weather as he replied. "Well, I kept dreaming about the bear. I woke up every time just before he got me. But the last time, he was so close I could feel his hot breath on my face!"

"What happened?"

Travis was reluctant to say. He thought for a few minutes as he watched the snow continue to fall. He guessed that nearly a foot and a half had piled up overnight, burying practically everything in sight.

"Well, tell me," his dad pressed.

"You're gonna think it's crazy," Travis paused with hesitation.

"Go on."

"Colter. . . " and he could say no more.

"It's okay, Bud. It's okay. No more jokes, okay?"

Travis was glad about that. He was hungry, too. "Something to eat?" he asked with a smile.

"Maybe some soup."

The conversation had allowed Travis to temporarily forget his father's condition, but the mention of soup jolted his memory. "Soup it shall be," he said as he opened the stove door to stoke the fire once again.

Without looking into the fire box, Travis grabbed a piece of the wood he had dragged in during the wee hours of the morning. He had begun to shove it into the stove when he noticed that the fire box was full. It was as though he had just put wood in it, but he knew he hadn't. He wheeled around and stared at the clock again. Perhaps he had read the time wrong when he first woke up. But he hadn't. It now read 11:50. Travis mixed the soup as his mind went to work. "Must have gotten up and didn't remember," he thought. "Or maybe it was Colter." His imagination was at work again. "No way! Naah, musta got up earlier," and he let it go at that. He poured some of the soup into a cup, grabbed a spoon, and turned to give it to his father.

The man took the cup, but Travis could see immediately that he was not strong enough, and he lacked the coordination it would take to feed himself. "Here, I'll help," he said as he took the cup back. Dad's inability to feed himself had answered at least some of Travis's questions about his condition. He asked anyway, as he raised the spoon to the swollen lips, "How you feelin?" It was a dumb question, he thought as he attempted to rephrase it. "I mean, better or worse?"

"Good soup," was the reply.

"No. I'm serious. It's not funny!"

"Pretty good," his father said, nodding his head. "Yeah."

As he raised and lowered the spoon, Travis analyzed that 'Pretty good' was a huge overstatement, to say the least. It was probably more like 'Pretty bad'!

When the soup was finished, Matt dozed off without saying a word. Travis put his open palm on his forehead. It seemed a bit warm, and Travis guessed that maybe his dad had a bit of a fever. He wondered if it was from the back injury, or maybe infection from the cuts.

Travis was worried. He knew that he needed a plan, but what could he do? Other than keeping his father fed, relaxed, and clean, what could he do? "Maybe I should go for help," he thought. "Maybe I should hook up the travois again and take off." It seemed like a great idea, but he remembered some of the hills and tight places they had ridden through on the way here. Now with the snow, it would be next to impossible to get a travois through. "No matter what I do, I'll need the horses," he thought as he headed out to feed them.

The snow was deep—as deep as Travis had estimated. And it continued to fall. Not as hard as it had been, but still hard enough to cut visibility down to forty or fifty yards, he guessed.

The horses were all still crowded in under the shelter, except for Buck. He was out eating the tall meadow grass. Travis smiled as he thought about how hard old Buck had worked, and he was always hungry anyway!

As he lowered the sack of grain from the tree, Travis wondered about Colter and the bear. Were they real? Sure seemed real. Or, maybe . . . ? It had to be real! But where was Colter now? Why didn't he show himself? "He could help me make a plan," Travis thought.

He needed a plan. His father was in need of medical attention, and even Travis knew that the sooner he got it, the better things would be for him. "Yes," he thought as he dragged the bag of grain through the fluffy, pure snow, "Colter would know what to do!" He wondered if the tall, wiry mountain man would show himself, or if he was only visible in his dreams. Travis felt a presence, but no one was anywhere near the camp, as far as he could tell. But, still, he could *feel* something!

After giving the horses a generous portion of the oats, he dragged the somewhat lighter bag of feed back to the tree and hoisted it up out of bears' reach. He didn't want any more trouble with those creatures! As he tied it off, he looked around, quickly scanned the visible country side for the beasts, then wheeled and ran for the tent. The thought of bears had scared him. About half way to the tent, Travis realized that. He stopped, turned around, and protested the fear with defiance. He wasn't going to run. He wasn't going to allow the fear to dominate his mind or his emotions!

"Got to be rational," he thought. "Gotta get a plan now. No sense in waiting or depending on Colter. I gotta do it. Colter's not real. He's been dead for over a hundred years. Just my dumb imagination again!"

He looked over at the monument tree with his partially carved name on it. TRA, it read. Now, instead of wanting to finish his name, he wished he had never started the carving. For that matter, he wished he had never even seen the tree! He could be in school now with Hal, and even Mrs. Goodman would be an inviting sight. But here he was—caught, stuck out here in the middle of nowhere! The middle of nowhere without a plan and, at this time, with very little hope.

The sight of the tree had set his emotions boiling again. He was ready to get an axe, chop it down, and burn it. But then he regained control of his thoughts and realized he was doing the very thing he had, only seconds before, told himself he wouldn't do. "Get a grip," he thought. "Stay focused. Get a plan."

He stepped back into the tent, again wondering what he should do. He had been up for over an hour now, and had no more of an idea about what to do than he had had when he first woke up. He thought about the old saying that, "Not having a plan is worse than having a bad plan," and decided that focus and clear thinking would be his first plan.

He crammed a piece of wood into the stove, glanced at his sleeping father, and dug into the licorice. As he chewed on the sticks of licorice, he thought about Smitty. "Maybe he's on his way back. Or, better yet, maybe some of the other campers he stopped to talk to are on their way out." Apparently no one had gone out yesterday. Surely, they would have stopped and read the note he had left. And no one would have ridden last night. "Maybe, maybe someone will be coming today," he thought. "But could they see the camp from the main trail?"

He didn't know for sure, but at least now he had a starting point for a plan. Something would have to be placed on the trail to get the attention of any passer-by. He thought for a minute, then reached for his journal and pencil. Quickly he scribbled out another note, grabbed his coat, and began to drag the big camp box down toward the trail. "No time to waste," he said to himself. "If I don't hurry, maybe I'll miss someone by only a few minutes."

His adrenalin was working, and in only a few minutes, he could see the trail. The box was much easier to move in the snow. It plowed a path down to the trail, where Travis parked it right in the middle so it couldn't possibly be missed. He tipped the box up on end and attached the note with a pin from the first aid kit. "They'll have to run over it if they come down this trail," he thought as he stood back and looked at it. "Not visible enough, though," he thought as he looked for horse tracks in the deepening snow. There were none to be seen, meaning no one had gone down this trail this morning. No passers-by meant hope to Travis that someone might still be coming, and even more hope for getting help for his father. "Better brighten it up. Make it more noticeable."

He headed for the tent on a dead run. Thrashing through things in the tent, he found an old fluorescent orange Winchester hunting shirt. That would make the box very visible. And it did. Now, for sure, the box would be sighted by anyone near the trail.

The rest of the afternoon passed by slowly. As hard as he tried, Travis could not make a decision about what to do. He thought about taking off with Skeeter and Annie at first light in the morning. He was sure he could find the way. And Skeeter had been here lots of times before. He would know his way!

Travis pondered the idea. He didn't want to do it. He prayed that help would arrive at the tent at any time, but it didn't. The thought of riding in the snow alone, not knowing for sure where he was going, struck fear in his mind. The fear made him think even more about planning a venture out into the winter wilderness.

"Maybe I should stay and take care of my father, sit it out and wait for help. Help will come. I know it will!" As he thought about all the pros and cons of staying or going, he could barely tell himself if he was making sound decisions, or if his thoughts were simply copouts caused by uncertainty.

Again, he felt terribly alone and chilled with fear. Right now, more than anything, he wanted his mom. She could comfort him and help him make a decision. No matter how hard he tried, he couldn't make one on his own. Every time a sense of duty and responsibility told him to go for help, fear told him to stay put and wait.

Travis wrestled with the challenge for hours, again losing track of time. It was nearly six o'clock when he looked at the clock. Realizing that his father had not said a word since he had eaten the soup, Travis jumped up, wondering if he were dead.

CHAPTER 26

The old matriarch had traveled to this spot in the valley every fall now for eleven years. She hadn't always held the rank which she now possessed but, nonetheless, it was an annual event. This year was different, though. It was much earlier in the season—nearly a month earlier than normal. She didn't know why she was here so soon, but she watched over her valley as others began to show up for the annual pilgrimage to the south.

As the days passed by, more and more followers came and prepared for the journey. Young and old—cows, calves, spikes, and even mature bulls gathered. They would follow when the queen led them out of the safety of the park. The followers were as nervous about the early gathering as their leader, but they trusted her to make the right decisions at the proper time.

Usually there was snow on the ground when they gathered at the rendezvous point, but not this year. It was warm during the days and hardly cold at night. Several thousand head had gathered now, but still there was no reason to leave. The only reason there had ever been for the elk to leave the safety of the park boundary was the deepening snow and the need for food to survive the harsh mountain winter.

There was no snow to prompt her now, though, so she waited, standing above her followers and admiring them. She didn't have a calf this year to follow her. It had been lost to predators early in the spring. However, she had several daughters and granddaughters in her immediate group. Some would be capable of leading the herd, but they respectfully waited their turns. They were a tight knit group, always watching out for each other.

On the third day, the wind began to blow, sending all to the cover and warmth of the trees. Nervous, though, the leader often stuck her head out, smelling the northern chill of the air. She knew she should leave the summer home, but did not yet have a physical reason to do so. Patiently, she waited for an excuse to travel.

The fourth day saw the wind leave. All gathered in the valley to play and feast, most forgetting the reason they were here in the first place. As darkness approached, the reason appeared. At first, there were only small squalls but finally, as dark set in, it became heavy snow.

The queen looked on, watching the snow with growing anxiety. She had an uneasy feeling that they should have left sooner, but justified her lack of action because she had never left before the snow. Some years, they had stayed until it was knee deep. Still, there was a feeling of regret. With so many depending on her, she hoped her choices were good ones.

The snow continued through the fifth day. First a foot of the white stuff piled up. Then, suddenly, there were two feet. She wanted to leave now, but many of her faithful were bedded in the trees in spots where they could not see, so she felt it was best to wait. She would wait for clear skies when all would have a chance to see her leaving. Then they would follow.

The sixth morning in the valley brought a glimmer of sunlight. The old cow stood up, pawed away the snow from a clump of grass, shook the snow off her back, and took a couple of mouthfuls of the lush green foliage. Then she headed south. The snow was belly deep now. She would lead the group out of Yellowstone. One by one, the followers fell in behind her, stretching the line out for nearly a mile.

The sun was only bright for a half hour or so, but it had given her the chance to fill her ranks. The annual migration to the winter feeding grounds had begun!

When she started out, she was not sure which trail they would take once outside of the park. Then, as the clouds rolled back in and the snow started to fall again, she knew she would have to use the ancient trail. It was not the safest of choices most years, as it was often lined with hunters. Recent trips had taught her and others to avoid this trail.

But it was the easiest one to travel, especially with the snow becoming so critically deep.

It was a chance she would have to take. Lives may be lost—a few here and there, perhaps even her own. But that seemed a better choice than using one of the steeper, more dangerous trails and risking the loss of the whole herd to the winter.

The group had traveled less than a mile and its leaders were already tired. Pushing the snow and breaking trail was hard work. The queen and five immediate followers stepped aside now and let others break trail for a while, until they became exhausted.

If all went well, in less than two days they would be safely inside the boundaries of the refuge.

CHAPTER 27

Travis reached down to grab his father's shoulders. Instantly he froze, realizing that he might cause even more injury by doing such a foolish thing as shaking him to wake him up. Instead, he placed his hand on the injured man's forehead. Travis didn't know a lot about these medical things, but he could tell by feeling that his father had a high fever. His forehead was burning. "Maybe infection," Travis thought. "Need to clean the wounds again. Probably should get him awake and feed him again, too."

As he began to remove the gauze bandages from his dad's face, he could see small pockets of pus in some of the cuts. Even Travis knew that this was not good. He would have to clean and wash them out with peroxide.

Dad's eyes were still closed, and remained so until Travis began cleaning his face, popping open spots that appeared infected. The first touch of the antiseptic caused the man to wince and growl with pain. He could barely moan, "What ya doin'?"

Once again, Travis replied, "Shhh. Cleaning infection. You got a terrible fever. Don't talk. Let me finish. Then we'll talk."

The odor was as bad as it had been the night before, but it didn't seem to bother Travis as it had previously. He was all business, scraping and cleaning every cut with the thoroughness of a well trained nurse. He was getting the wounds clean, but not wasting any of the first aid materials. He was well aware that he might need them later on.

As he finished, he stared down at the mummy-like face and almost began to cry. He didn't, though. Instead, he laid his head against his father's chest and let the tears flow silently. He wasn't crying on the outside, but inside. It helped to relieve some of the pressure and fear he was feeling. This had gone on for some five to ten minutes when Travis noticed his father was trying to put his hand on his shoulder to comfort him, but he couldn't raise it high enough to do so.

Travis used the sleeve of his flannel shirt to wipe the tears from his face. Then he looked up at his father and asked, "What should I do?"

His dad slightly shook his head from side to side, not speaking. Travis knew the gesture meant, "I don't know."

"I set the box with a note in the middle of the trail, but no one came by today. Nobody."

Matt acknowledged again with a head shake.

"The way I see it is, no one knows we're in trouble and you need help," Travis said as the tears began to flow. He wasn't crying aloud, but he wanted to. He held it back as best he could. He had to be brave now for his father's sake, he thought as he began digging through the supplies for some more of the powdered soup. When he found it, he ripped the bag open and dumped it into a small kettle of water heating on the stove.

Matt must have sensed that the soup was cooking. He motioned for Travis to come to him. Travis approached and looked him sternly in the eye. Matt gasped for breath and then asked, "How deep?"

Travis knew what his father wanted to know and replied, "About two feet."

"Stay here, warm. They'll come." With that, Matt had expended most of his energy.

Travis had deciphered the mumbled message. He mulled over it in his mind as he turned away and tended the soup. That would be the easy thing to do, and probably even the right thing. But what if no one showed up for days, or even a week or two? What if . . . ? Then it came to him. What if he stayed and no one showed up and his father died? He couldn't live with this idea, and now knew that he had to go for help. He thought about how much worse his father had gotten in one day, and rationalized that, if he continued to lose health at this rate, he may at best have three or four days left to live.

Travis spent the rest of the afternoon getting ready for his trip down to the trailhead. "I'll take Skeeter and Annie," he decided. He fed the horses again in the deepening snow, always feeling the presence of someone watching but never seeing a soul. Of course, there was also the hope that someone would come down the trail, but that thought dissipated along with the daylight. He had hoped to see someone, but the emptiness and loneliness only grew greater as the hope decreased.

Travis continued to have the feeling that someone was watching him. The presence of another was so strong that, before he entered the tent for the evening, he walked a circle around the camp, never losing sight of the well lit tent. He wasn't sure what he was looking for—maybe a set of tracks or some kind of evidence that someone was around. He had hoped to find something, yet nothing appeared. Finally he dismissed the feeling as only a mirage, a figment of his boyish imagination. "The dream triggered all of this," he thought. "I oughta be spending this time getting ready to leave in the morning rather than chasing dreams and hoping for help, which does not exist, to come."

As hard as he tried to dismiss the feelings of the presence, he couldn't completely rid himself of them. There was always that small ray of hope, adding unrealistic reality to the dream and his thoughts. After a time, he decided it was only the dream haunting him. It didn't matter a lot, though, he figured, as he prepared a pack to be ready to leave at daylight.

Travis calculated he could make it out to the trailhead in six to eight hours and back with help in just over a day. The trail had been easy to follow before the snow. He only hoped that it would be visible with the snow cover.

The evening was spent stacking wood and moving the travois into position so that, if Dad had the strength, he could keep the stove fired up from his homemade traveling bed. Travis packed enough food for himself for two days. He wanted to keep his load as light as possible, yet have a bit extra just in case. He didn't want to think about getting lost or losing the trail, but he knew that it could happen. His rations would consist of jerky, licorice, dried fruit, and the trail mix his mother had made.

Travis decided not to tell his father that he was leaving, even as he fed him this night. With all the moving and work he had been doing, Dad surely knew something was up. But Travis figured there was no sense in worrying him until morning. "Yeah, I'll tell him right before I leave," he thought. He headed for his bag to get a good night's sleep before he had to leave his sanctuary in the mountains.

As he began to crawl into the bag, Travis noticed his journal and picked it up. Nothing had been written in it since before the attack. He thought he had done a good job of writing in it, but remembered how much of a burden it had seemed, just to take the time to do it. Now, though, he knew that it wasn't such a big deal. He wished that his biggest worry was to have to write a few pages about all of the fun he was having! The assignment seemed trivial at this point, and he took up the pen and began writing a detailed account of the tragedy which had befallen him. And, even though he wouldn't want to be laughed at or teased, he wrote about the presence of Colter, or, what he believed could be Colter. He even wrote about the dream.

As he was finishing, he wrote, "I'm leaving at daylight to get help. Hope I can stay on the trail. I guess I don't know if what I'm doing is right or wrong, but I have to do something. I can't sit here waiting for someone who may not show up for weeks. I would survive, but by then it would be too late for my father. If someone is reading this journal, please see to it that it gets to my mom. If, for some reason, I don't make it back, take good care of my father. I don't want to think about the worst, but it seems as though the worst has come to be real. Tell Mom, Dad, and Jess that I love them, and I'm trying to do what is right."

As he turned the lantern down for the evening, Travis closed the journal and began to think about what he had written. It scared him a bit. He worried that leaving might prove to be a dumb thing to do. But, what else could he do?

The day had seemed very short, he thought, as he watched the reflections of snowflakes flashing past the side of the tent in the dim light.

CHAPTER 28

Travis slept better this night. He didn't dream about the bear or Colter. Rather, he dreamed about staying on the trail and finding his way out of the wilderness. At one point, he could not see the trail and could not decide which way he should go. He noticed a person walking toward him. He turned Skeeter toward the approaching figure and pushed ahead, only to find. . . nothing! No man on foot, and no trail. Only endless snow and trees.

He looked around and realized he had no sense of direction. He reached into his pack for his compass, but it was gone. There was nothing in his pack! No food, no compass, nothing to start a fire. Nothing! He wondered how he could be so dumb as to leave camp with an empty pack, but he had done just that.

"How long have I been riding?" he wondered. "An hour? A day? Two days?" He didn't know.

Suddenly there was the figure walking toward him again. He pushed Skeeter even harder this time, thinking maybe it was his brother, Jess. But, as he got closer, the person just disappeared. "Jess could find me," he thought. "Jess will come. He'll come!" And that's how Travis woke up—hollering for Jess.

It was still dark out, but he decided he would get the horses ready to go, and clear the snow from the top of the tent. As he worked at lugging the tack and preparing the camp for his absence, he thought about his latest dream. He wondered if maybe he should not go, after all. "Maybe someone is trying to tell me something. Maybe I shouldn't leave." The dream had created doubt and confusion, but Travis fought off the ill feeling about leaving. He was a stubborn young man, and his mind was made up.

Saddling up Annie and Skeeter was a lot more work than he had remembered. As he thought about it, he realized that this was the first time he had ever done the job by himself. Hal or Jess or Dad had always helped before. He sure wished one of them were helping him now!

The snow was deeper now, pushing three feet, Travis thought as the low light of morning on this dark day began to show itself. Now he had only to tell his father his plan and he could be on his way. He trudged to the tent, dragging his feet and plowing the snow that was more than waist deep on his small body. He didn't really know why he was doing this—only that he was a young boy, and for twenty or thirty seconds he had forgotten about the danger and seriousness of his dilemma.

As he pushed the tent flap open and entered, reality hit him in the face. He had never been faced with having to openly tell his father that he was going to disobey him. "Maybe I should just go, and not tell him," he thought as he heated some coffee, water, and more soup. But he knew he couldn't do that. He had to prepare his wounded father to spend at least a day and a half on his own.

It was quickly approaching daylight, enough that he would be able to ride. He didn't want to waste any time. As he awakened his father, he had the feeling that the man could see right through him and already knew what Travis was about to tell him. But he didn't. He had no clue. Travis removed the bandages from his father's face as he waited for the soup and water to warm up. "I should have started earlier," he thought, "maybe even stayed up last night." As he examined the infected wounds, he realized that this would take time—time he didn't really think he could spare. But the wounds had to be cleaned. "Should have stitches," he mumbled as he worked.

Matt nodded weakly and asked, "What's up?"

Travis stopped working for a second, looked his father directly in the eyes, hesitated for a moment, and then couldn't speak. He thought to himself, "I'll wait 'til after he eats. Don't want to upset him now."

"Not much," was his delayed response to his father's question. "Woke up early and couldn't go back to sleep." He began to put new wraps on the mauled face.

"Feelin' any stronger today?" There was no reply. Matt didn't want to say, and Travis didn't really want to know.

"Fever's still with ya," Travis commented, trying to make small talk as he began to feed his father.

Finally, when the soup was just about gone, Travis couldn't hide his intentions any longer. He set the spoon in the kettle and blurted, "I've gotta go for help. I know you said to stay and wait, but I can't."

Even through the pain, Travis could recognize the disapproval in his father's eyes, and hear it in his voice as he started to speak. But Travis cut him off as tears began to flow—not tears of fear this time, rather tears of caring and love. "Don't talk. Save your energy and listen. I can't stay here and hope that someone comes along. I mean, get real! You need help and I'm the only one who can get it for you. You know I'm right. You gotta know!"

Travis could see a glassy, almost tearful look in his father's eye as he muttered, "No." But it was to no avail. The boy's mind was made up and his conviction to go for help was stronger than ever.

Once again, he cut his father off. "Here's my plan." Then he blurted out the details. "Everything you will need is in arm's reach. Save your energy. You'll need all of it you can muster to get wood into the stove. The food and water you will need is here under my bag." Travis had covered his dad with his own sleeping bag when he had awakened earlier in the morning. He had placed licorice, jerky, and dried fruit under it , along with a water canteen, so that Dad could easily reach them. "I know it's not the best food, but you gotta make it work. There's Sterno and a lighter here, also, if you can't get wood into the box. It's not terribly cold out, so don't use the Sterno unless you absolutely have to. I'll be back. And don't start a fire in here. Be careful!"

Travis was rambling on. He realized he was treating his father like a child and decided to cut it short. After all, Dad knew what to do. Sitting around and nagging at him was only burning daylight. "Just do your best and stay warm for a day, and I'll be back with help."

With those words, he started to step out of the tent. Then he looked back at his father. He turned and lunged back inside. He knelt and gave the man a gentle hug so as not to hurt him. With a creak in his voice, he said, "I love you."

Matt looked up at his son with tears in his eyes. He mustered one word, "Stay."

"I can't. And you have no right to make me stay here and watch you die. I'm not scared." With these words he got up, opened the flap once again, and left to get the horses.

As Travis began to climb up on Skeeter, he noticed the pack he had tied on Annie. Remembering his dream, he walked over to her and checked his equipment. He confirmed that he had a compass, lighter, Sterno, food, and the other gear that he hadn't had in his dream. Only after he had checked the entire pack did he mount Skeeter and head for the trail.

The snow was still quietly falling. "Over three feet by now," he thought as he looked back at the tent disappearing from his sight.

CHAPTER 29

Skeeter plowed through the fluffy white snow with ease as the trio moved down toward the south end of the meadow. After a hundred yards or so, the tent had faded out of sight. Travis's sanctuary was gone. There was nothing to protect him from the elements now except his clothing, his partners on this journey—Skeeter and Annie, and his knowledge.

The trail through the meadow was easy to follow, only because the grass on each side of it was so tall. It looked like a perfect, white highway about two feet wide. He hoped it would remain this way for the entire day.

Travis was scared and worried. Oh, he had told his father that he wasn't scared. Indeed, at that time, he had no fear. But, as his journey began, fear and doubt had begun to build. He wondered if maybe he should have listened to his father and stayed. It would be easy to turn around and follow his trail back to the tent, but he didn't. He just kept on going farther and farther into the white wilderness.

Several times, he stopped Skeeter and thought about turning around, but each time he jabbed the horse in the ribs and continued on. "It's like the dream," he thought. "I can't go back. I can't turn around. It's just like I couldn't leave when the bear was lurking in the dream. But why?"

Remembering the dream also made him think about Colter. He hadn't felt the presence for some time now, and he wondered about it again. Since it had disappeared, he assumed it had only been a figment of his imagination. He wished it were real, but knew that it was not. "Dreams just aren't real," he told himself. "They're only like wishes.

And I need real help!" After all of the joshing and ribbing he had taken, who would be better to wish for than Colter? It made sense to him now, why it had been Colter who had saved him in the dream. And it disappointed him, knowing that it had not been real.

Even while he was thinking about the dream, Travis wondered if he were doing the right thing. "How will Dad make it? Can he keep the fire going?" he wondered. "What if he accidentally sets the tent on fire?" Negative thoughts flowed through his mind. Before he had left to get help, he had only thought about why he should go. Now that he was on the trail, he could only think about why he should have stayed.

The trail was not as easy to follow as it had been earlier. They had been traveling for about half an hour now, and Skeeter was already beginning to sweat. With the horse showing signs of tiring, more doubts were cast in Travis's mind. He began to wonder if he was traveling in the right direction, even though he was pretty sure that he was. "How could I not be?" he thought as the trail entered a small patch of timber.

Skeeter plowed through this area with greater ease. The pine boughs above them held large amounts of snow, and sagged with the ever present threat of dumping their loads on the travelers. The snow would build up on them to the point where they could hold no more weight. They bent down lower and lower until the snow finally dropped. Once in a while, one would drop a load of the white powder very close to the three travelers, but somehow it always missed the target in its bombing attempt. That is, until the lad and his horses headed into the third patch of timber.

Immediately upon entering, the entire side of a tall pine tree took aim and dumped fifty or sixty pounds of snow on Travis's head! It wasn't funny, and it didn't feel good either, he thought as he tried to dig the icy wet stuff out from around his neck and dust himself free of it. He had no more accomplished this task when another load fell and hit him. "Not such a direct hit this time, though," he thought to himself. "This is gonna be fun!" He had a notion to turn back, but he pressed on, wondering what lay ahead.

The snow continued to fall. Travis wondered whether or not he was making good time. Had he traveled enough distance at a pace that would get him to the trailhead before dark? He had no way of knowing or judging how far he had traveled, though, because of the extremely limited visibility. There were no distinguishable landmarks to travel by—only the fifty yards or so that he could see in each direction. Although the trail was still visible, it seemed to be more and more difficult to see as the snow began to fall even harder.

He came to a spot in a small opening on a mesa where the trail forked, going off in two different directions. Travis stopped Skeeter and tried to make a decision as to which fork to take. He didn't remember seeing this split in the trail on their way in to the campsite, but maybe he hadn't been paying much attention then.

Skeeter was sweating hard now and needed a break, Travis thought as he tried to make up his mind which way to go. Both trails entered the dark timber about ten yards in front of him. He couldn't decide! "How could I not remember this?" he asked himself in a state of near panic. He wished he had help now, but he had no one. He felt the same terrible, empty loneliness he had felt that first night after the mauling. His gut was empty—completely hollow. His heart began to race. A wrong decision could be fatal!

Suddenly he felt, once again, as though he were being watched or stalked. The presence of another was near. "Man or beast?" he wondered, as his small heart pounded even harder. Instinct told him not to move. Motionlessly, he scanned the area around him, looking for anything that seemed out of place. But again, nothing could be seen. "Is it the bear?" he wondered. "Is it lurking just inside the timber, waiting for me to ride into an ambush?" Or, would he wait in this spot for the beast to attack, just as he had in the dream? His mind raced. "Perhaps I wasn't standing on top of the elk. Maybe I was sitting on Skeeter." He looked down at Skeeter's sorrel colored neck and mane and thought, "Yes, I could have mistaken Skeeter's hide for an elk hide!" It would certainly explain why he had been on top of the "elk" in the dream.

Slowly, he slid his hand down toward the rifle scabbard, clumsily unbuttoned the strap, and began to pull out his father's rifle. He knew that the bear would appear any second, and he needed to be ready when it happened. "I'll only have one shot," he thought as he lifted the rifle and pulled the bolt back to jack a shell into the chamber.

Travis thought he saw a dark object moving toward him through the vision-obscuring snow, but he couldn't tell for sure. "Maybe my imagination again," he tried to convince himself. "Or maybe it's the bear, just like in the dream." He could definitely see a form taking shape just inside the timber.

He was raising the rifle to take aim when he heard a voice say, "Put that thing away before ya kill a tree, Boy!"

Travis didn't know who it was, but he obeyed, fumbling even more to unload the rifle and get it back into the scabbard than he had to get it out. When he finally got the rifle back in its place, he started to jump down off his mount to see who was coming out of the timber. "Perhaps someone looking for me," he thought hopefully. But he froze with one leg in the stirrup and the other leg halfway over Skeeter's back when he looked down. Only a few feet away stood the tall, lanky mountain man who had saved him in his dream! Travis couldn't say a word as the man looked up at him. "This can't be," he thought. Finally, he managed to choke out one word, "Colter?"

"Yes, I am," came the reply. "John Colter, to be exact!"

Travis was dumbfounded. He couldn't believe this was happening. "I must be sleeping," he thought. Meekly, he spoke, "Thought you were a bear."

Colter roared, "I'm much prettier than any old bear!"

Travis smiled as Colter asked, "What in tarnation you doing out here? Trying to kill yourself, or what?"

"What do ya mean?"

"Just what I said."

"Well," Travis hesitated, "I'm going to get help for my father. He's hurt. Attacked by a bear."

"I know. I know. But you need to turn those ponies around and get back to camp."

"No," Travis replied. "I have to get help. I mean, he's really hurt!"

Colter's eyes hardened as he told Travis a second time to follow his trail back to camp. Travis's patience with the man was beginning to wear thin. He was a determined boy, and he had decided he was going for help.

"Okay," Colter said with a smirk on his face. "Try this. Which one of these is the main trail?"

Travis didn't know, but quickly decided he would choose the one on the right. He pointed to it.

"No," Colter replied. "Try again."

Without thinking, Travis pointed to the trail on the left.

"No," came the reply again.

"What do ya mean?"

"You're not on the main trail, Boy. You left it about a half mile back!"

"How could I have done that?" Travis wondered.

"Yeah, at the rate you're going, and using the trail you're on now, I figure you'll get to the trailhead in two days if you survive. But you probably won't. Go on if you want to, but I'm goin' back to camp."

"You could show me the way, couldn't you?" Travis asked in a tone that almost made him sound like a beggar.

"Yeah, I could. But I'm not gonna. Now, did you hear that?"

"Why not?"

"You're a stubborn one, aren't ya? Mostly it's because you can't leave your father alone. And . . . you . . . know . . . why!" With that final exchange, the mountain man started to head back toward camp, following the cleared trail which the horses had made. Travis hesitated only briefly, then turned Skeeter around and began to follow.

Colter walked for about five minutes, never looking back to see if Travis was following. Suddenly he roared, "Thought you was goin' for the trailhead!" He laughed a loud, defiant, sarcastic laugh.

Travis didn't say a word, but his mind thought. It thought that Colter was little more than a loud, arrogant, bossy wise guy. But, at this point, even that kind of personality had promise. It somehow left Travis with a feeling of comfort.

CHAPTER 30

The two moved on for some time not speaking. It seemed as though each was daring the other to speak first, but neither would say a word. The tension grew inside Travis until he could stand it no longer. He began to talk. "Who are you?" he asked.

"I told ya who I am," Colter replied. "What are ya? Deaf? If you wanted to talk, Boy, ya shoulda just said, 'I wanna talk.' Come up with this foolish line, 'Who are ya?'" Colter mumbled. "Who do ya think I am? Queen of England? Yeah. I'm the Queen of England, Boy!" The mountain man roared again with that fakish kind of laugh.

Then the loud, arrogant man said in an almost normal, pleasant voice, "I'm sure glad you talked when you did. I couldn't hardly stand that quiet anymore. Truth told, if you'd a waited a minute longer I'd a started talkin' first. Guess I'm a bit thicker skinned than you, huh, Runt?" The mountain man let out a teasing chuckle.

Travis was not amused. Matter of fact, he was mad. Fighting mad! He told himself that he didn't have to take this kind of abuse from anyone, and he wasn't going to! He tried to muster up an intimidating voice, not thinking before he spoke. "I don't need your help, cause I'm not lost." He was losing confidence with each word he spoke. Then he thought, "Oh, no! Why did I say that?"

Colter stopped in his tracks and turned around, almost bumping Skeeter in the head with his arm. He looked up at Travis and said, "Boy, there may be even less hope for you than I thought. You're lost. Oh, you're lost. But you ain't bright enough to know it. And, you know what? That's the worst kind of lost!"

Travis tried to reply, maybe even apologize, but Colter cut him off as he began to speak. "You oughta be thankin' me for followin' ya this mornin' and gettin' ahead of you after you left the good trail. Had to run for darn near a mile to cut ya off. Lucky I even followed at all. Didn't figure in a hundred years a runt like you would leave camp in these conditions."

Travis was awe-struck. What gave this mouthy stranger the right to talk to him in this tone? He wanted to attack the mountain man, but he couldn't. He could think of nothing to say. The glare in Colter's eyes was far too intimidating for a twelve-year-old to stand up to.

The silence didn't last long, though, as Colter spoke again. "You committed the ultimate sin today, Runt. You left your partner in the mountains. And you don't do that unless you're sure the man can make it while you're gone. Never! Period! That's all there is to it."

Once again, Travis spoke without thinking. "I had to leave to get help. He'll die if . . . "

Colter cut in, "He'll die if you leave him alone!"

"If he'd a shot the bull on opening day, none of this would've happened."

Colter spun around again and replied, this time with a touch of feeling in his voice, "You don't know that. You can only think that. Listen to me, Boy. This isn't his fault, and it surely isn't yours either. It just happened, that's all. It just happened." He turned then and walked on, through the trail which was beginning to fill with snow again.

Travis followed, thinking that maybe this mountain man did have a heart. His last sentences had not mentioned the word 'runt', and he did seem to be concerned about Dad. But, who was he? Or, what was he? Is he a ghost of the real Colter? Or, perhaps, an angel? Or a real live mountain man? Travis pondered these ideas for a while, but could not come to a conclusion.

Suddenly Travis remembered that Annie was saddled, and that Colter was walking. "Want to ride Annie?" he asked.

"That would be nice, except these horses are gonna need all of the strength that they have later tonight when ya head for Jackson."

Travis was dumbfounded. Was this man crazy, taking him back to camp and then telling him he was going to leave tonight? "What about my dad?" he asked.

"What about him?"

"You said I shouldn't leave him."

"You won't."

"I got lost during the day. How will I find my way at night?"

"What is this? A thousand questions, or what?" Colter sarcastically replied. "You'll have a guide."

"You?" Travis questioned.

"No."

"Then, who?"

"Your guide is a bit more experienced than me, Runt." Colter laughed again.

Travis didn't like being toyed with this way. Why did Colter have to call him Runt, anyway? Just when there seemed to be a chance for a friendship to develop, he had to go and use that word again—Runt! Travis just couldn't figure this guy out.

Most of the rest of the ride back to camp was without conversation. Travis figured they must be getting close when Colter asked, "Why didn't ya finish carvin' your name in the tree?"

"I hate that tree! I'd chop it down before I'd carve on it again!"

"Have to say, you were doin' a fine job on it. How do you hate a tree, anyhow?"

By now the tent was in sight, and Travis was relieved to see it. It gave him some comfort to know that he would soon be inside where it was dry and warm again. Yet, he wondered why Colter seemed so friendly and nice one minute, then cold and hostile in his very next sentence. He didn't feel scared of Colter, but he didn't know if he trusted him, either.

Travis's delayed response to the question was, "I came here to get a trophy bull elk, not to whittle on some dumb tree."

Colter laughed. "Oh, so now the tree's dumb. I see." He finished his statement with a "Hmmm . . ."

Standing directly in front of the tent now, Colter said seriously, "You listen to me. Feed the horses and get ready to travel. Not heavy.

Pack light. Feed your father and keep him warm, but be ready to go. I don't know when for sure, but some time tonight."

Travis listened, but at the same time he wondered, "Is this idea sane? Leaving at night?" Then he asked Colter, "You gonna help?"

Colter laughed and said, "No. I got some things of my own to tend to, Runt."

He had to say that word "Runt" again! This time, it infuriated Travis and he fired words back at the mountain man. He was no longer intimidated as he yelled out, "Maybe I don't want to go. Maybe I'll stay here!"

Colter didn't look back as he walked away, plowing through the snow. But Travis heard his reply. "Get ready!"

"For what?" Travis screamed. "For an old man to get me lost in the dark?" Deep down, Travis didn't want Colter to leave but, in his rage, he hollered again, "Go on! Leave! I don't need your help, anyway!"

He threw the reins down in the snow and hustled into the tent, knowing that the fire had probably gone out and regretting his final words with Colter. He couldn't change them now, but he sure wished that he could. Maybe he realized that Colter was right. He couldn't leave his father in the cold.

Nothing in the tent had changed. The fire in the stove was out. Dad had not even tried to put wood on it. Perhaps he hadn't been able to. Travis checked his father's breathing. Then he built a fire, wondering all the while if Colter was coming back. He hoped that he would, but he still wondered if leaving at night was a good idea.

As he tended to the fire and checked his father more carefully, Travis wondered who this guide was that Colter had talked about. He began to worry even more about Colter not coming back, and found himself dressing again to go out. He wanted to track down the mountain man and apologize for being so mouthy.

He ran right past Skeeter and Annie, who were still standing exactly where he had left them. He followed in Colter's footsteps, hollering for him to wait up, but his summonings were to no avail. Over and over he hollered, but Colter was gone. "Either gone, or just not answering," Travis thought. The tracks went the same direction as Travis and his father had gone each morning to hunt. He ran, following them for nearly a quarter mile by his estimate, until he had run out of breath and felt exhausted. He called for Colter one last time, huffing and sucking the thin mountain air, but still there was no answer.

Somberly, he turned around and headed back for camp, wondering again if he had made the man mad enough to desert him. Reasoning that Colter was a man of at least some honor, Travis figured he'd be back—back with the guide he had talked about. "I'll be ready when they get here. I'll be ready," Travis thought.

And the snow continued to fall.

CHAPTER 31

Travis wasted no time preparing the five horses for the journey. After giving them each a generous portion of feed, he saddled Annie and Skeeter and put the panniers and pack saddles on Dusty and Flick. Buck wasn't loaded at this time. He would have the most important job, pulling the travois. Travis watched the old horse as he ate the cubes and oats. He was sure Buck had no idea about what was going to happen sometime during this night. He only hoped that Buck would be up to the task. Now he was finished with his outside chores but, before he left, Travis put his arms around Buck's neck and said, "Eat well. You'll need the energy."

Then he headed for the tent to dry himself out, warm up, and prepare himself and his father for the long ride. Once inside the warm tent, Travis began scavenging through all of the gear, throwing equipment into two piles. The things he would need went into one pile, and what could be left behind in another. It was an easy job until he came to the video camera. After several minutes of agonizing debate with himself, he decided to leave it. Every ounce lighter the load was would make it that much easier for the horses. The pile to go was limited to food, clothing, first aid supplies, an axe, and fire starting materials.

After everything, including his father, was ready to go, only then did Travis lay back on his bedroll. He had taken it back from Dad when the tent had warmed up. Now he chewed on some licorice as he reflected on his day and prayed that Colter would show up tonight. He wondered and worried as his eyelids grew heavy, and he dozed off into a peaceful sleep.

It was dark outside when he awoke, startled, thinking he had slept too long. Thinking maybe he had missed something, but still not knowing what that might be. Immediately he wondered if Colter had come back. Apparently he hadn't. At least, not yet. Besides, it couldn't be too late in the evening, he thought as he fumbled around for the clock. Even after finding it he didn't know, because he had forgotten to wind it. "How could I have forgotten?" But, he told himself it didn't really matter anyway. It was night, and Colter had said, "Tonight." Travis would wait.

His attention switched to his father and he felt a bit ashamed for a moment. Since meeting up with Colter, he had barely even thought about Dad. At this moment, Travis figured that it would maybe be good to try to wake him and get some nourishment into his stomach. Travis didn't have to wake him, though. When he turned the lantern up, he could see his father's eyes looking at him.

"Came back," Travis heard him say. His voice sounded stronger.

"Yeah," Travis replied. "I gotta feed you and talk." He stayed close by the stove making the soup again, only this time he talked as he cooked.

"I was lost, Dad. Colter found me. And we're leaving tonight."

There was no reply, only a puzzled look on his father's face. Then he muttered, "Colter?"

"I know it sounds crazy, but he was here and he's coming back tonight with a guide. And, if he does, we're leavin'." Travis expected some kind of argument from him about leaving, but none was offered.

After his father had finished sipping down the soup, he looked up at Travis and said, "Colter . . . go . . . after the elk." There was a relieved look on the man's face. He had exhausted his energy and closed his eyes to relax, and then sleep again.

Travis could make no sense out of the words, "Colter go after the elk." What did it mean? Was Colter looking for elk, Travis wondered. Perhaps it was the fever talking. Most likely, he thought, because it surely made no sense to him!

After sitting and waiting for some time, Travis began to worry. Was Colter coming back? It had been dark for several hours, and there was no sign—no sign of Colter, or of the guide he had talked about.

Travis chewed on licorice, put wood on the fire, and tried to find busy work to keep himself occupied. He didn't want to go out into the night and travel in the vast darkness, yet he believed it was necessary. Necessary for his father and, for some unknown reason, necessary for his own self-esteem. He had to make this journey! But he couldn't start without Colter. Here he sat with the snow piling up ever deeper, and Colter wasn't showing up.

It was perhaps three hours now since dark. Travis needed to do something, so he decided to go outside and look around. He didn't know what good it would do, but at least he would be doing something. Quickly he put on his hooded sweatshirt and a jacket, slipped on his boots and gloves, and stepped out of the tent to look around.

He didn't look far because, as he headed around the corner, he met Colter! The mountain man was plowing snow as he came at a slow trot, nearly running Travis over. He had a huge bundle on his back, and . . . what was this hanging off to each side? Travis immediately recognized the huge set of antlers that Colter was carrying. "Are they from the old dead bull?" Travis asked as Colter dropped them and the pack to the ground.

"No, they're from a live one!" Colter laughed. "Of course they're from the dead one. Seemed awful important to you, so I brought 'em back. And, I tell you one other thing. If you want 'em, you load 'em. I done did all the work I'm gonna for one night, and I ain't touchin' them stinkin' horns again!"

"Don't worry," Travis replied. "You won't have to touch . . . them . . . again."

He smiled as he thought to himself, "Wow! Now I'll show 'em! Yup, they'll know I'm not lying or exaggerating one bit!" His thoughts raced on and on about how great it was to have the horns. They were enormous—the kind every hunter dreams of. "Perhaps even a record book set," he thought. "These horns are awesome!"

Colter cut in on Travis's gloating and asked, "Ya ready to go? I mean, travel?"

"Yup. Been ready for hours."

"Good. Did ya pack light?"

"Yup."

"Horses ready?"

"Yup." Travis had a positive answer for every question. And then he had a question of his own. "Where's that guide you talked about?"

"They're coming," Colter replied.

The word 'they're' raised another question in Travis's mind. "What do ya mean, 'they're'?"

Colter answered with his usual sarcasm. "Well, when I was a boy, I guess 'they' meant more than one. In this case, about a thousand."

Travis laughed. "Yeah, a thousand guides. In my dreams, maybe!"

At the very moment he finished that sentence, Travis picked up on some movement out of the corner of his eye. Not ten yards away, a cow elk plowed through the snow. She was moving slowly but, nonetheless, moving. She was followed by another, and then another, and yet another. The leader had, by now, faded out of sight into the snowy night, and Travis watched motionlessly and silently as the elk continued to file by, one behind the other.

Finally he spoke. "How many you suppose there are?"

"About a thousand," Colter chuckled. "And it's not a dream."

For a moment, Travis didn't understand what he was talking about. Then, suddenly, it hit him. A thousand elk. A thousand guides. "No way! They aren't the guide you're talking about, are they?"

"Yup."

"No . . . . No . . .," Travis replied. "I'm not following a herd of elk."

"Don't, then. But I'm tellin' ya, they'll find the way to Jackson and clear a trail for you. And they'll take an easier route than you or I would."

"No!"

"It's up to you," Colter said, sounding as though he were becoming disgusted again. "But, if you're wantin' to save your father, you better get with it."

Travis wasn't sure what to do. He needed to get his father out to a doctor, that was for sure. But, to go after a herd of elk? Then it hit him. Dad had told him to do just that! Travis recalled the garbled words his father had spoken earlier, "Colter . . . after the elk." Dad had been telling him to follow the elk!

"Okay," Travis said as he walked toward the horses to fetch them to the tent. "I'll be ready in ten, maybe fifteen minutes."

"You sure change your mind fast," Colter grumbled. "I'll help."

"Thought you weren't gonna help."

"I lied. Can't help it." Then the mountain roared, "I don't have to help!"

"It's okay," Travis chuckled. "As my mom would say, 'Just a little white lie.'"

The two loaded the horns onto Flick. Then Colter picked up the pack and walked inside the tent. By the time Travis got in behind him, curious to find out what the pack was, Colter had Matt half wrapped in a huge moose hide. Travis must have looked puzzled. "This will keep him warm. Well, at least warmer," Colter explained as he finished tucking the huge black hide around Matt, being careful not to hurt him. After that was done, they backed Buck in and hooked him up to the travois again. Now they were ready!

Travis stuck his head outside the tent, shining the light in the direction of the elk. They were still moving past in single file. "We'll wait for about half of 'em to go by before we join in," Colter said.

Travis figured they had fifteen, maybe twenty minutes before they would cut into the line of elk. Quickly he surveyed the tent, looking for his journal so he could scribble a note for anyone who might happen by. "Maybe Smitty," he thought as he wrote: "Took father and followed the elk." He hadn't thought about taking the journal with him, but after he had finished writing and torn the page from it, he shoved it inside his shirt underneath his hooded sweatshirt. As he zipped his jacket, he looked up at Colter. The mountain man smiled and said, "Good Idea!"

And the snow continued to fall.

CHAPTER 32

The trail the elk had made was narrow, but clear, as Travis and Colter and the horses cut in. The elk seemed to be a bit skittish and scared at first, but after a few minutes they grew used to the intruders. A cow's white rump patch showed only a few feet ahead of Annie, and another's nose followed only a few feet behind Dusty. It was as though the men and horses had become a part of the caravan.

Travis led the way. He was leading Buck, who was pulling the travois. They were followed by Colter riding Skeeter and leading Flick, who was carrying the provisions they might need, along with the majestic set of horns. Dusty brought up the rear, carrying the feed and a few supplies.

The snowflakes continued to float down from the heavens as the group moved at an almost intolerably slow pace. Travis could see a little bit as his eyes adjusted to the darkness, but he kept his flashlight handy, shining it ahead and then back every once in a while just to make sure Colter was still following.

Neither Travis nor Colter spoke for the first hour or so. Travis's feet started to get cold from sitting motionless in the saddle for such a long time. The cold stung and bit at his feet, but he didn't say anything. He just kept riding.

It was Colter who finally spoke, breaking the silence of the dark night. "Better stop and check your father."

Travis stopped immediately and jumped off Annie, causing immense pain to himself as his cold, nearly frozen feet hit the ground. It felt as if needle-sized icicles were being stuck into them. "Oohhh . . . "

he moaned as he moved toward the travois, not noticing that Annie was still following—following the elk.

Colter pulled up the hide which covered Matt's face. Travis asked, "Are you cold, Dad?"

"No," was the reply. It was weak-sounding, but it was good that his father was warm, Travis thought.

"Feet cold?" Colter asked Travis as he covered Matt again.

"Yeah."

"Walk for a while. That'll help."

The elk behind them had stopped, but those in front of them had continued to move on. Colter tied the reins around Skeeter's neck, grabbed Buck's lead rope, and they moved ahead to catch up with Annie and the lead group of elk.

"Sure make a nice trail, don't they?" Colter laughed.

"Yeah," Travis replied with concern. "I just hope they know where they're going."

"I think they know," Colter chuckled.

"That's a big word."

"What?"

"Think. You *think* they know. And why are they movin' so slow?" Travis asked as he began to pick up the sight of Annie's rump just ahead of him.

"Think about it, Boy. The ones right at the front of this train are really workin' to push that darn snow out of the way. Must be three and a half feet, or more."

"Yeah, guess so. How far do ya think we've gone?"

"Maybe a mile," Colter replied. "Maybe."

"It'll take a week!"

"No, just 'til sometime tomorrow."

"Which direction we goin'?"

"Hmmm . . . " Colter replied. "Don't really know. Does it matter?"

"Are we lost?" Travis asked, showing great concern.

"No, we're not lost. We're followin' the elk!"

"We're not lost, but we don't know where we are," Travis mocked with just a touch of sarcasm. "We're following a bunch of animals. Makes perfect sense to me."

Colter laughed. "I like your spunk, Boy, but, don't worry. As long as the elk can move, they'll get us there. And one other thing. Up here in the mountains, being lost is a whole new experience. It's different."

"What do ya mean?" Travis asked, waiting for Colter to explain his way out of that line.

"Well . . . you can only get lost if you have somewhere particular that you're going and you can't find your way."

"So, I suppose you've never been lost then, huh?" Travis chuckled.

"Nope," Colter replied.

"No?" Travis smirked. "Well, you must be like a walking compass then, huh?"

"Nope," Colter sassed back. "Just never been lost much. Didn't really have anywhere particular I was goin', so how could I get lost?"

"Never had anywhere to go?"

"Well, sometimes I was goin' somewhere—east or west or north or south, I guess. The dark got you nervous, Boy?"

"No," Travis answered, realizing that he had forgotten how dark the mountains were and how, only a few days ago, the darkness and the unknown of the night had frightened him. How quickly he had out-grown that fear!

The walking had warmed his feet and, for the first time since they had joined the caravan, Travis noticed that they were in the timber only once in a while for short spurts in and out of the trees, occasion-ally crossing logs. The travois straddled the trail well enough that it even crossed the logs with ease. Travis only hoped that the ride and the cold were not too hard on his father.

His thoughts were interrupted by Colter. "Hey, let's ride these horses. My feet are gettin' tired. Feel like I been walkin' all day. Guess I have, though, haven't I? No thanks to you, Boy."

Travis smiled as he crawled back up onto Annie's back. He could hear Colter mumbling something to Skeeter. The arrogant mountain man had become a regular chatterbox, seemingly not concerned about anything. Travis was glad to have him here. "But, what a bad attitude!" he was thinking as he could hear Colter still talking to Skeeter.

At times, Travis could tell that the trail was steep as the horses strained to pull themselves and their loads up the hills. He worried about Buck most of all. He had the toughest load, and he was old. Travis didn't know how old, but he knew Buck had made many of these trips before. He hoped the horse had one final trip in him.

The snow continued to pile up, ever deeper and deeper, as Travis worried and Colter talked on. The night seemed never ending, and the pace was too slow. The night was not only long, but wet and cold—especially cold when they were riding the horses. The travois pulled hard and, even though Travis couldn't see Buck very well, he could sense that the horse was tiring. But Buck was a good animal and he continued to pull and follow, working hard to keep up.

The two would ride for about a half-hour and then walk for a while, pressing on. Each time they stopped to walk, Travis would get some oats out of the feed bag and give them to Buck. The horse took them and ate each time, but with little vigor. Travis hoped that the oats would give Buck the energy he needed. He figured it was kind of like himself eating a candy bar. But the strategy didn't seem to be working. It was simply a very difficult pull for the old horse.

Colter finally spoke. He suggested that maybe they should hook the Travois to one of the other horses. Travis insisted, though, that Buck was the only horse that could do the job. "He's the most trustworthy."

Colter argued, "What are they gonna do, other than follow the trail?" Travis was persistent, though, and Buck continued to pull the load.

Travis was tired now, too, and each time he crawled up on Annie's back he fought sleep. His eyelids were heavy and his mind would almost relax to the point of sleeping, but he fought against it, knowing that dozing off could be very dangerous for him. Falling asleep could mean freezing on a night like this, and thus, he continued fighting the urge.

The first rays of daylight began to show themselves. Travis and Colter were walking again. The snowflakes were still large and steadily falling, showing no sign of retreat. Travis looked up at Colter and, for the first time all night, saw his face. Icicles hung from his beard and moustache. "Your face cold?" he asked in wonderment.

"No," Colter replied as he took a glove off and pulled the ice off his moustache by partially thawing it with his fingers and pulling at the same time. Travis thought that it looked cold, but Colter insisted that it wasn't.

As it became lighter, the next thing Travis looked for was Buck. His concern for the horse was great, and a close look only confirmed his suspicions. Buck was tired, sweating heavily, and straining hard with his load.

"How much further?" Travis asked.

"Don't know," was Colter's response.

"Well, guess then. I gotta know!"

"Five, six hours, probably."

"When we get to the top of the hill, we gotta stop and let Buck rest."

"Better to put the load on one of the others." And the debate started again.

Upon reaching the top and inspecting the horse further, Travis could no longer argue. The travois poles had rubbed sores on Buck's hind quarters. Now he knew he would have to put the travois on Flick, who had carried the lightest load all night long. She could finish the trip with the heavy load.

They let the horses eat as the two of them worked. They first unloaded Flick, then unhooked the travois from Buck. After hooking Flick up to the unit and making sure her hind quarters were protected with some pads under the poles, Colter turned to begin loading Buck with the gear and horns.

Travis nearly tackled the mountain man, stopping him abruptly. He looked up with tears in his eyes and said, "No. Buck can't carry anymore. We'll split the gear and put a little on each horse."

"What about the horns?" Colter asked.

"We'll leave 'em," Travis replied, fighting back his deepest emotions.

"You sure?"

"Yeah. I'm sure." Travis threw the horns to the side of the trail, grabbed Annie's lead rope, and moved on.

As they rode, Colter could feel Travis's despair. Then he spoke. "For such a small boy, you have, in one day, turned into quite a young man. I know giving up those horns was hard to do, but you did right."

Travis just stared back at the magnificent rack, half buried in the snow. "Guess they'll never believe me now, will they?"

Colter spoke more quietly now. "All that matters is that you know. You know what happened. You know what you had—or could've had. You have it in your heart now, Boy. You know why you were here and why your pa didn't shoot that bull the first day. You may not realize it now, but in your heart, you know."

"Maybe. My dad . . . Buck . . . the horns . . . . What next?"

It had been daylight now for a while, and Travis stopped often to check on his father and Buck. Each time, he would look at his father first and then feed Buck some oats, hoping that this would give the old mountain horse the energy to continue on. Buck was wet and stiff. His flanks quivered as though he were cold.

Travis and Colter walked a lot now, too, not talking much. Talking took energy, and the entire group was tired now. It seemed hopeless to Travis. The snow continued to fall, covering the earth in an ever deepening blanket of the white, fluffy stuff. Even though they stopped often, each time they started again, they would quickly catch up to the lead group of elk. "The elk must be tired, too," Travis said in despair as he looked up at Colter.

"Yeah. They're tired."

"Hard push, huh?"

"Yup. Uphill, deep snow. They're tough, though. They'll get ya there!"

But Travis wasn't so sure now. His enthusiasm and determination had vanished. "Maybe," was his meager reply.

His attention was diverted back to Buck as he watched the faithful partner now struggling to keep moving. Travis could see that putting one foot in front of the other and moving forward was more than the horse could manage. "Should've listened to you," he blurted out to Colter. "Should've changed the load to Flick earlier. Should've changed!"

Colter didn't speak. He just listened. Buck almost stopped at times, and it made Travis frantic. He would pull on the lead rope, knowing that he wasn't helping but needing to do something. Each time, though, Buck managed to muster the strength to go on. Barely, but somehow, he continued.

Finally Travis looked up at Colter and sobbed, "He ain't gonna make it, is he?"

Colter still didn't speak. Rather, he looked down at Travis and shook his head slowly from side to side. Travis knew that meant 'no'.

Trying to be strong, he looked up again and sucked up all of the strength he had. "Buck's been good. He's done a lot. Walked right up to where that bear was. Always been dependable. Never let us down. And now, *I've ruined him!*" He continued to speak, getting quieter with each word. "Let's take a break and see if he can go on after a rest."

Colter finally spoke. "That's a good idea." This time he got the oats for Buck.

They rested for half an hour or so. Then Colter said, "We gotta move on. Can't be much farther, but it must be noon or later already."

"How much farther?"

"Don't know. Mile or two, I'd guess."

"Only a mile or so?"

"Snowin' so hard I can't really tell. But once we top this hill, I think it's down to the lake and there's the road. Just don't know if this is the right hill or not."

Travis looked puzzled, but he had renewed hope—a hope for Buck. "Well, let's go, then," and he prodded at the tired old horse. Buck moved, but he seemed stiffer. Travis's heart sank. He knew it was a longshot now.

Travis again pulled Buck. At times, he even pushed—pushed to the point of exhaustion. He was struggling to catch his breath. He hadn't even noticed the cow elk lying only a few feet away from him when he heard Colter command, "Enough!"

As he looked up to respond, he saw the elk lying there, half in and half out of the trail. Steam was pouring off her sweaty body. Colter spoke before Travis could. "If we're gonna make it today, this might be a good place to leave him."

"Don't want to."

"Let him stay and rest with the old cow. If she gets up later, he'll follow."

"Why is she here?" Travis questioned, wondering about the cow.

"Same as Buck. Old, overworked, and tired."

The look on Travis's face told Colter he didn't understand.

"Well, young man, I guess she's the queen, the matriarch. Probably the first elk you saw go by the tent last night. She's been leading the way, breaking trail since Yellowstone. She's a lot like Buck. She's worked too hard and, right now, she can't go on. But she's done her job, like Buck did his. She led the way and, though she might not survive, the rest of the herd will."

Travis looked at Colter with his glassed up eyes. He stomped out a spot in the snow beside the old cow who was too tired to move. Then he said, "Buck did his job, too, didn't he?"

Colter grabbed the feed bag off Dusty and poured it out in the spot Travis had stomped out for Buck. If they rest for a while and eat, they'll find the energy to make it out."

Travis knew that was a pretty big "if," but he knew it was his only option. He pushed Buck into the cleared out spot. Then he hugged the faithful old horse, jumped on Annie and rode up the trail, not looking back but feeling bad—feeling bad because he knew it was mostly his fault that Buck would probably lay there and die.

CHAPTER 33

Travis's heart had sunk—hit bottom. He had no faith in himself, Colter, or the elk. He rode in the front now, not saying a word. He climbed the hill, pushing to catch up with the herd. Suddenly he noticed that the snow was getting lighter and the sky was getting brighter. A renewed hope surged through him as he rode out of the clouds and onto the top of a sunshiny hill. He could see the tops of other mountains miles away. The cloud bank below him spread out in all directions.

Something in his heart jumped and soared through the bright clear blue mountain sky, soared straight toward the sun—the sun he hadn't seen for days. Now he not only saw it, but he felt the warmth of it on his cheeks. That feeling of warmth added to the renewal of hope within him. He knew now that Colter was right. They were close—close to the road now. Below them, down in the clouds, would be the lake Colter had talked about.

Travis stopped Annie. There above the clouds and snow, he sat looking at the splendid peaks of the Tetons to the west of him. Now he knew, for the first time, what his father had meant about hunting being an experience with nature. Colter had told him that he knew, but he hadn't felt it. Not until now. The cloud bank and snow blanket below him took on the look of a bed of cotton and, though he didn't have a camera, he knew that this picture would never be lost. For a second he wondered, "Could this be heaven?" He sat in awe for several minutes, knowing he had never seen a more beautiful landscape.

Travis was still admiring the view when he felt a hand touch his shoulder. "Well, it's not even a mile down there, Partner. Some of the elk are probably already to the road."

"Think so?"

"Yup," Colter affirmed. Then, almost groping for words, he added, "Guess this is where we part."

"Part? What do ya mean?"

"It's only a bit farther, and I'm stayin' here."

"Do ya have to?"

"Yeah. This is where I belong."

"I won't get lost?"

"No. Besides, help's comin' up the trail now. Better get goin'!"

"Thanks for everything. And take care. Maybe someday we can actually share a fire and swap stories." Travis paused, then reached down and shook the big man's hand.

"Yeah, that would be good. Maybe even carve that name of yours in the tree."

"Maybe," Travis replied. "Maybe. How will I find you?"

"That's my camp your dad uses, you know."

"I knew that," Travis said smiling. "*I knew that!*"

"Go on now, before I get all teared up here," Colter said with a touch of the sarcasm Travis had become used to. "Go on. And remember, you've lived what most others only ever dream!"

Travis jabbed Annie in the ribs and headed down into the clouds and snow below them. Suddenly, he heard a loud voice roar, "Don't worry about Buck. I'll send him down!"

At the same time, he heard another voice yelling, "Travis!" He looked ahead to see his brother, Jess, coming up the trail toward him.

"Jess!" he hollered back as he rode up beside him. He jumped off Annie and tackled his brother in the snow, giving him a big old hug.

"How's Dad?" was Jess's first question. "And how'd you get the idea to follow the elk?"

"Dad's okay, and Colter . . ." Travis stopped. "Well, I don't think Dad's really okay, but he's alive. Needs a doctor bad, though."

Jess had to see for himself. As he began to unwrap the moose hide, he asked Travis where he had gotten it.

"Col . . ." Travis started to reply, but couldn't finish.

His father, with his eyes open, finished for him. "Colter," he said. "Colter."

Jess nodded his head in understanding. Then he said, "We better get goin'."

Travis turned and looked back at the vision of the mountain man in the trail behind him, waving goodbye. He knew that his brother would never believe that it was real. But when he turned around again, he caught Jess staring back at the same spot.

"What is it?" Travis cried tearfully.

"It's a . . . Oh, nothing. It's crazy!" Jess responded.

"No, tell me. Did you see? Did you see Colter?"

"It's . . . it's crazy. But, yeah, I did. At least, I think so."

Travis turned around to holler "Thanks!," but Colter was gone. He wanted to say a lot of things but, for now, he said nothing. He knew his secret about Colter would be safe with Jess because, like Colter, Jess was probably a part of these mountains. After all, how did Jess find him? Why was it Jess? There must have been dozens of others looking for him. How could Jess have found him if he were not a part of it in some way?

The two of them turned and headed the caravan down the hill and followed the elk again.

"How'd you know where I was?" Travis asked as they neared the road.

"Smitty managed to get through by radio. Said Dad was hurt."

"Oh."

There were twenty-five or thirty people waiting at the road. Travis caught sight of his best friend, Hal, jumping up and down and waving. There were also rangers, and an ambulance. And there was the one person Travis most needed to see. He jumped off Annie for one last time, and ran to throw himself into his mother's outstretched arms. He began to blurt out words at an incomprehensible rate. His mother hugged him tightly, held his head against her shoulder, and quietly whispered, "Shhh . . . later."

That night Travis lay in a soft, warm bed, pondering the events of the last week. He wondered about Colter and the elk. "The elk are probably near the refuge by now," he thought. Then he said a prayer: "Thank you, Lord, for sending me Colter, for keeping Dad alive, and for sending the elk to guide us. And look after Buck. I hope they all sleep well tonight. Amen."

Give the Gift of

Partners in the Wilderness

to Your Friends and Colleagues

CHECK YOUR LEADING BOOKSTORE OR ORDER HERE

❑ **YES**, I want _____ copies of *Partners in the Wilderness* at $15.95 hardcover or $7.95 paperback, plus $4 shipping per book (Wyoming residents please add 80¢ sales tax per hardcover book, or 40¢ per paperback book). Canadian orders must be accompanied by a postal money order in U.S. funds. Allow 15 days for delivery.

My check or money order for $_____ is enclosed.
Please charge my: ❑ Visa   ❑ MasterCard
                   ❑ Discover   ❑ American Express

Name _____

Organization _____

Address _____

City/State/Zip _____

Phone_____ E-mail _____

Card # _____

Exp. Date_____ Signature _____

Please make your check payable and return to:

JETBAK Publishing
1829 Bluegrass Circle, Cheyenne, WY 82009

Call your credit card order to: (866) 815-3015
Fax: (307) 266-0033